DANCING
IN THE RAIN

DANCING
IN THE RAIN

•

Amanda Harte

AVALON BOOKS
NEW YORK

PRINTED IN THE UNITED STATES OF AMERICA
ON ACID-FREE PAPER
BY HADDON CRAFTSMEN, BLOOMSBURG, PENNSYLVANIA

For Donna Marie Tayntor, with thanks for so many things, but especially for being my friend as well as my sister-in-law.

Chapter One

October 1917.

It was not the first mistake she had ever made, but it just might be the worst. Carolyn Wentworth stared at her reflection in the mirror as she pinned the starched cap onto her head. Her face looked the same as it had every other day: heart-shaped like her mother's, with her father's deep blue eyes and golden blond hair. Her appearance hadn't changed, but the way she felt most definitely had. Never before had she experienced the horrible sinking sensation that now lodged in her stomach. Never before had she been convinced that she had made an irreparable mistake.

Carolyn frowned as she turned away from the mirror. What on earth had convinced her that she could do this? Why had she believed that she, who had never worked a day in her life unless you considered planning a ball at the country club work, would be able to succeed at an occupation that many women considered daunting? Perhaps everyone at home was right, and it was insanity that had provoked her actions. Perhaps.

Carolyn shook her head as she grabbed her last clean apron. She would wait until she crossed the courtyard before she put it on. That, she knew, was the only way it had

a prayer of remaining clean for more than a minute. She
shook her head again. Coming to France was not a mistake.
It couldn't be.

Though her sisters had predicted that she would regret
her impulsive decision, Carolyn had refused to listen to
their nay-saying. It was true that she knew little of her
destination other than the fact that it was home to some of
the most beautiful castles in the world. It was also true that
she knew nothing of the war that had ravaged Europe for
years, save the reports in the *Canela Record*, which were
sketchy at their best. Her sisters were right about that, but
what they hadn't realized was how strongly Carolyn had
believed in her decision. And now?

She shivered, as much from nerves as from the cold that
seeped through the stone walls of the castle that was now
her home. From four thousand miles away, France had
sounded beautiful, the cause glorious. Reality, Carolyn had
discovered, was far different. Reality was a countryside
decorated with hedges of rusted barbed wire rather than
evergreen shrubs. Reality was towns whose beauty had
been devastated by years of battles. Reality was seemingly
endless rain and its companion, mud.

Carolyn hated mud. Though it rained in Texas, the soil
near Canela was sandy enough that puddles were rare and
mud even less common. She frowned as she reached for
her cape. Wouldn't the old biddies at home laugh if they
could see her now? Carolyn Wentworth, the girl who spent
half her clothing allowance on pretty dancing shoes, was
wearing boots that a lumberjack would be proud to own
and slogging through mud that, no matter what she did,
slopped over the boot tops and slid down to her toes, making her feet squish with each step. The same girl, whose
party frocks were the envy of her friends, now spent her
days in dismal gray cotton uniforms with white cuffs and
collars that were impossible to keep clean. Even the shape-
less white aprons, the sole part of her costume that was

laundered regularly, were stained within minutes of starting work.

Oh, yes, the biddies would laugh, but they'd also nod. "I told you so," one would announce to the other biddies, the way she had that day when the Ladies' Auxiliary had met at the Wentworth home and no one had realized that Carolyn was close enough to hear their words. "She might be the prettiest of the Wentworth girls, but she certainly wasn't blessed with brains." "A beautiful but useless decoration," another had said.

They were wrong! Carolyn hurried down the steep stone staircase, pausing momentarily when she reached the ground floor. She could hear the rain pounding, and even though it was only a hundred feet across the courtyard, that was enough to drench her. So what? The men she was going to see had endured far more than cold, soaking rain.

Carolyn straightened her shoulders and prepared to dash across the courtyard. The Ladies Auxiliary was wrong. Her sisters were wrong. The whole town of Canela was wrong. She might not be as bright as her sister Martha, as clever as little Emily, or as brave as their brother Theo. But she was still a Wentworth, and she was not—she most definitely was not—useless.

Carolyn sprinted across the expanse of mud that had once been a formal garden, her eyes focused on the wooden door leading to the east wing. Tonight she would write to her sisters, describing the elegant chateau that served as staff housing as well as a hospital, rather than alarming them with tales of the suffering she had witnessed. In the meantime, she would show everyone that she was not useless. Perhaps that would dissolve the knot of fear that had taken residence in her stomach.

Carolyn had come to France to prove that it wasn't just Theo and Ed and all the other men who had joined the Army who could make a difference. If this was truly the war to end all wars, she would do her part. And right now that part meant proving that she hadn't made a mistake. Carolyn Wentworth was going to be the best nurse's aide anyone in Goudot, France had ever seen. She wrinkled her nose as a raindrop slid down it. Why stop there? She'd be the best aide in all of France, not just in this town thirty-five miles southeast of Dieppe.

She tugged the heavy door open and let herself into the east wing. What had once been a grand ballroom and several smaller reception rooms had been turned into an operating theater and wards for the non-ambulatory patients. Carolyn donned her apron, then forced a smile onto her face and sauntered into the first ward, pretending she was walking into the Canela Country Club for the most important dance of the season. Despite the heavy boots, her step was light, and she let her skirts sway ever so gently. Sodden cotton didn't drape like silk, but even the slight swirl added to the illusion. Perhaps if she could convince herself that this was not a mistake, the men would never know how close she was to fleeing like a frightened rabbit.

"How are my favorite beaux today?" Carolyn asked. The low murmur stopped, and she felt twenty pairs of eyes focus on her. "As you can see," she said with a rueful glance at her mud-spattered skirt, "this is not Goudot's driest day." Thank goodness, her voice sounded as carefree as if this were indeed a party and the men were her dancing partners. Maybe those years of planning parties and learning to treat even the most difficult guests' demands gracefully were more valuable than she'd realized. At least her horror at the suffering that surrounded her wasn't audible. Now, if only she could keep smiling, it wouldn't be visible, either.

"I told you she'd come," one man announced to the patient in the bed next to him. Though Carolyn could see only the back of the second man's head, it was swathed in a bandage. He must be a new patient, someone who had been brought in after her shift ended yesterday. Perhaps in a day or two she would know the men's names, but yesterday the wards had blurred into a single image of nameless men.

Another patient made a show of consulting his watch. "She's five minutes late, Henry," he said to the man with the head wound. "I was sure she didn't want to see us no more."

Still another man nodded. "C'aint blame her. This place is enough to make a man sick, let alone a purty gal."

Carolyn tried to keep her smile from fading. Though she had thought that she had camouflaged her feelings yesterday, it was obvious she had not. These men had realized that she was appalled by the sights and sounds of the hospital ward, and they had been betting on whether or not she'd return. How shallow she must have looked! Here they were, soldiers who had been wounded, and she—an ablebodied woman—was so weak that she couldn't face them. Perhaps the Ladies' Auxiliary had been right. Perhaps she had been useless. But that was about to change. These men deserved the best care, and she would give them nothing less.

"Now, gentlemen," Carolyn said with the smile that had never failed to charm the young men of Canela, "don't tell me y'all would hold it against a girl if she spent a couple extra minutes primping." As she had hoped, the men exchanged grins. Carolyn lowered her voice to a conspiratorial level. "I shouldn't tell you this. My granny would say that I was destroying the mystery, but the fact is, I wanted to wear my best perfume for you, and I had to look everywhere to find it."

The man named Henry gave a triumphant crow. "I told you! You fellas were wrong." He turned his head toward the doorway where Carolyn still stood, and her heart plummeted with pain as she realized the nature of his injuries. "C'mon over, honey. Let me be the first to smell that perfume."

Carolyn kept the smile fixed on her face as she approached the blind man. Although Henry could not see her, the other patients could. "Here I am, Mr. Phillips," she said, reading the name on the chart at the foot of his bed. She stood at his side, hoping that the scent that she had so liberally sprayed on her wrists and throat would overcome the smells of the sickroom.

The room itself was lovely, its walls covered with a delicate green wallpaper, its oak floors gleaming from years of polish, its windows long and perfectly proportioned. Even crowded as it was with beds, the room was still beautiful. What was not beautiful was the stench of illness, medicine, and harsh cleaners.

"I'd be honored if you'd call me Henry," the man said. He was older than the other patients, perhaps in his thirties, his accent telling Carolyn that he was English like her new roommate.

"I couldn't do that, sir." She stuck a thermometer into Henry's mouth. "My granny wouldn't approve. She always said a girl shouldn't be too familiar with a gentleman the first time she met him."

One of the other men chuckled. To Carolyn's relief, the mood in the ward had lightened. Laughter, she had heard, was a healing force. Perhaps she could use that to help these men.

"Say, Nurse, can you settle an argument for us?" The man who asked the question lay two beds away from Henry.

"I'll try."

"Tell my buddy here the right way to say the name of this here town. He says it's *go dot*, but them Frenchies just laugh when we say that."

Carolyn shrugged. "They laugh at my Texas drawl, too. Don't ask me why, but the French don't pronounce the last *t* in Goudot."

"Did you say *goo dough*?"

"That's right."

The soldier turned to his friend. "Fellas, I reckon we can remember that. We've sure got a lot of goo here, and we're Doughboys. Doughboys stuck in the goo."

When they stopped laughing, the man next to Henry asked Carolyn to write a letter for him. Writing letters was one of Carolyn's talents. Unfortunately, she was far less skilled at the tasks that were her primary reason for being here.

Today was a little easier than yesterday. She spilled less of the water when she washed their faces and hands, and the patients that she helped eat did not look as if they had taken a bath in their food today. Perhaps with a few more days' practice, she would have mastered those chores. But the last chore . . . Carolyn tried not to let her revulsion show. There was no chance that she would ever enjoy emptying bed pans. Not even the scent of her perfume could keep her from wrinkling her nose at them.

"I reckon this don't smell like a country club." To Carolyn's mortification, one of the patients chuckled at her distress.

"Maybe not," she agreed, "but my dancing partners in Texas weren't as gallant as you gentlemen are."

"I shore would like to dance with you," the man replied.

Carolyn knew that his wish was unlikely to come true, for he had a compound fracture of his left tibia. Looking for a way to ease his worries, she started to say, "My granny . . ."

"Carolyn?" At the familiar voice, Carolyn raised her head. Helen Guthrie, the nurse who shared with Carolyn the tiny third-floor room that had once been a scullery maid's quarters, stood in the doorway, her face ashen. "As soon as you're finished . . ." She gestured toward the hallway behind her.

Though Carolyn did not know the other woman well, she was familiar enough with illness to know that something was wrong. "What can I do?" she asked a minute later, when she'd made her excuses to the patients.

"I need your help," Helen said. She had looked ill when seen from a distance, but close up, her pallor was alarming, her face unnaturally white against her dark brown hair, her eyes clouded with pain. "Hollow Heart is back, and he needs me in the operating room," Helen continued, her voice weaker than normal. It wasn't, Carolyn was certain, only the prospect of working with the man who was reputed to be the most difficult of the Army physicians that caused Helen's pallor. The woman was ill.

Carolyn raised one eyebrow. "I know it's not polite to say this, but you look awful."

"I feel awful," Helen admitted. "I can't keep any food down, and my legs don't want to support me. I can't go in there." She shuddered as she glanced toward the operating theater.

Unsure what Helen thought she could do, Carolyn asked, "Do you want me to ask Miss Pierce to assign another nurse?" The head nurse was strict, but everyone agreed that she was fair.

Helen shook her head. "There isn't anyone else. The fighting near Ypres is worse, and we got another trainload of patients last night. Right now there are more wounded than the doctors can handle." Helen gripped the wall as another wave of pain washed over her. "Everyone's on duty. That's why I need you."

Carolyn reached out to steady her roommate. At just over five feet tall, Helen felt tiny compared to Carolyn's own five and a half feet. "What do you mean?" She wrapped her arm around Helen's shoulders.

"I need you to take my place."

Carolyn shook her head. "You know I can't do that. I'm a nurse's aide, not a nurse." If she had difficulty with bedpans, how would she handle surgery? "I don't know anything about operating room protocol."

"Please, Carolyn." Helen's English accent became more pronounced as she pleaded. "Think about the men in there. They need you."

It was crazy. It wouldn't work. She would get sent home in disgrace for impersonating a nurse. Carolyn started to shake her head, but as she did, she pictured Theo or Ed lying on a stretcher, waiting for a doctor. How could she not do whatever was possible to help all the men like her brother and her fiancé?

"What about Hollow Heart?" she asked, referring to the doctor whose reputation terrified the nursing staff.

The gleam she saw in Helen's eyes told Carolyn that Helen realized she had decided to help her. "He probably won't know the difference. He doesn't look at us nurses, anyway. We're just another instrument that he needs—not real people. Besides," Helen asked, "what can he do to you?"

"He could fire me." The image of the notorious Dr. Hollow Heart throwing her out of the operating room rose before Carolyn. She could picture the man, tall and as lanky as Ichabod Crane, pointing a bony finger at her as he ordered her to leave. Then she laughed. "You're right, Helen. He can't do anything. You can't fire a volunteer." She gestured toward the door. "Go back to bed. I'll do my best."

And, crazy as it was, Carolyn was grinning as she walked toward the operating room. How much worse could this be than emptying bedpans? She had survived that, and she would survive this. After all, this was a chance to prove that Carolyn Wentworth was more than a decoration and that coming to France had not been a mistake.

Her smile faded when she opened the door and she paused for a second, trying to regain her equilibrium. She had been in the operating theater the day she arrived in Goudot, but that had not prepared her for the scene before her. The room had been empty when Helen had shown it to her on their impromptu tour. At the time, Carolyn had been jarred by the juxtaposition of flocked wallpaper and a gleaming parquet floor with sturdy iron beds and tables covered with instruments. Today she felt as if her senses were being assaulted. The voices of a dozen doctors and an equal number of nurses mingled with patients' groans, while the odor of carbolic acid failed to overcome the stench of illness. And in the midst of what appeared to be barely controlled chaos was the man she sought.

There was no question about which of the doctors was Dwight Hollins, more commonly known to the nursing staff as Dr. Hollow Heart. Only one man stood alone, pacing the floor. Only one man had a scowl etched onto his face. As Carolyn entered the room, he glared at her. With an ostentatious look at the clock, he said, "Good afternoon, Nurse."

"Good morning, Doctor," Carolyn corrected him. She wouldn't let this man intimidate her. He was, after all, just a man, like all the others. His legs were encased in the same knee-high boots, the same woolen uniform. Like the other doctors, he had slipped a white linen smock over his jacket to protect it during surgery. That was no surprise. What was a surprise was that he bore no resemblance to Ichabod Crane.

Dwight Hollins wasn't as tall as she had expected—perhaps an inch under six feet—nor was he lanky. This man was well muscled, and if it weren't for the scowl, his face would be a handsome one. His eyes were hazel, and though his hair was covered with a cap, Carolyn knew from Helen's tales that it was brown.

"Is it still morning?" he asked, his words dripping with disdain. "Or perhaps it is morning again? I've been waiting long enough that that seems possible."

Carolyn looked around. The other doctors and nurses were so engrossed with their own patients that they seemed not to notice her. Thank goodness. No one had recognized her as an aide and was going to demand that she leave.

Perhaps she could get through this after all. The first step was to placate the doctor. His nurse was late. Even though she was not responsible, there was no denying that. "I'm sorry."

The scowl deepened. "Don't apologize to me," he said, his tone somehow managing to be both frosty and yet burning with sarcasm. "It's the men here who deserve your apologies." Dwight Hollins gestured toward the stretchers that lined the perimeter of the room. It was a measure of how many wounded had arrived that the patients were here rather than being in a ward, waiting for surgery.

Laughter, Carolyn again reminded herself, could heal. She held out her skirts and curtseyed as if she were greeting royalty. "My apologies, gentlemen. My granny warned me that vanity was a sin and that I shouldn't spend so much time fixing my hair, but she also told me that first impressions were important. I ask y'all, what's a girl to do when she gets conflicting advice?"

As she had hoped, several of the patients laughed. Dr. Hollins did not. "If you're ready now," he said, his eyes darkening with something that looked like anger, "perhaps we could do our jobs."

"Certainly, Doctor." Carolyn tried not to think about the charade that she had begun. Somehow, some way, she had to make this man think that she was a nurse.

He uncovered the makeshift bandage on the first patient's arm and nodded as Carolyn took her place next to him. "Scalpel," he ordered.

Oh, no! There were half a dozen instruments on the tray. One of them was surely a scalpel, but Carolyn had no idea which. She froze.

The doctor held his hand out, then turned to glare at Carolyn. "The one on the right," he said, his voice as cold as ice. "Might I suggest that you spend less time trying to charm the patients and a bit more helping me."

She *had* been trying to charm the patients, but not for

the reason Hollow Heart thought. She started to protest, then stopped. So what if he believed she was frivolous and vain? That was preferable to having him realize that she had never before touched a scalpel. "Yes, Doctor," Carolyn said as sweetly as she could. "It won't happen again."

"It had better not."

And it did not. Carolyn soon learned that Dr. Hollins had a habit of glancing at the instrument tray before he requested an item. If she watched carefully, she would see what he wanted. After the first few times, she reached for the item and placed it in his open hand before he had finished asking for it. The second time that happened, though he made no comment, his tone seemed to warm ever so slightly. After that, it became a challenge for Carolyn. She tried to anticipate the doctor's needs, retrieving a suture or a bandage and handing it to him before he could speak. This was a game she could play and win. Even better, it served the very important purpose of helping keep Carolyn's mind off the men they were treating. If she focused on the instruments and Dwight Hollins's face, she was less aware of the twisted limbs and torn flesh and the men who suffered so greatly.

Many of those men were awake while the doctor treated them, and so Carolyn forced herself to keep a smile on her face. She would look at each one and give him a special smile, pretending he was the man of her dreams, the one who had escorted her to a ball at the country club. In her fantasy, they were dressed in formal clothing, and she wore a fragrant corsage. Though she smiled at the men and occasionally touched one's hand to reassure him, she never spoke to them. That might disturb the doctor's concentration. And if there was one thing Carolyn had quickly realized, it was that the doctor took his work seriously. So very seriously.

She glanced down at the ring on her left hand. Her sisters had told her that Ed was too serious for her, that she'd never be happy marrying a man like him. If Martha and Emily thought Ed was serious, they should meet Dwight Hollins. Compared to him, Ed Bleeker was a veritable comedian.

When the next patient was brought to them and the doctor uncovered his leg, Carolyn tried not to wince. Fragments of bone protruded from flesh so badly mangled that she could not see how it could ever heal. Though it was one of the most difficult things she had ever done, she smiled at the young man.

The doctor did not smile. "Chloroform," he said firmly.

Carolyn tried not to think about the reasons he wanted to sedate this patient. She wasn't here to think. She was here to help the doctor and by helping him, to help these poor men. As she held the soaked gauze over the patient's nose, she smiled brightly. The man returned her smile.

"He won't be smiling when he wakes up with only one leg."

Carolyn's hand began to tremble as the implication of the doctor's words registered. He was going to amputate the man's leg. She bit the inside of her cheek, then closed her eyes when she realized Dwight Hollins expected her to assist him. She couldn't! It was one thing to hand him instruments, to help him remove shrapnel and suture wounds. It was far different to cut off a man's leg. She couldn't!

Sensing her fears, the doctor fixed his gaze on her. "Is something wrong?" he demanded.

Everything! her mind shrieked, but she forced down the bile and said as calmly as she could, "Nothing other than a moment of pity for this man."

"He needs your help, not your pity." No wonder they called him Hollow Heart; the man had no emotions. He might be a skilled physician—and Carolyn had heard that he was one of the finest doctors in the Army—but he lacked basic humanity. How could anyone be so cold? She might have thought that it was a reaction to the destruction that surrounded them, a way of insulating himself from the constant suffering, but Helen had told her that the other doctors were far more human. What had made Dwight Hollins this way? Why didn't his heart ache as hers did?

Carolyn flashed her bright smile at the doctor. "I'll give this man both help and sympathy," she declared as the saw bit into the shattered bone.

Afterwards, Carolyn knew it was a blessing that she could recall none of the details of the surgery. She attempted to play the same game she had before, to watch Dwight's eyes and anticipate his needs. Sometimes it worked. When it didn't, he seemed to understand and would point to the instrument he needed. Somehow they finished the amputation. By the end of the day, they had treated more soldiers than Carolyn could count.

When their shift was over, Dwight Hollins nodded briefly as he removed his cap and smock. "Not bad, Nurse."

Carolyn felt blood rush to her face. For years, people had praised her beauty and her grace. Men had showered her with compliments. Women had told her how they envied her her golden hair, the eyes so dark a blue that they could only be called sapphire, and the heart-shaped face that her sisters wished they had inherited from their mother. Though those compliments had all been fervent, none had touched her the way Dwight Hollins's three words had.

Carolyn started to smile. Somehow she had survived the day without Dwight's realizing that she was an imposter, that she had never before done anything like this. Somehow she had managed to help the doctor, and in doing that, she had helped the men. Carolyn's smile broadened. The people at home were wrong. She was not useless! She had proven that. And maybe, just maybe, coming to France was not a mistake, after all.

Chapter Two

Dwight rolled the portable screen next to the bed. Though the other men in the ward would be able to hear him, the screen provided this patient a semblance of privacy. It also reduced distractions, and that, Dwight knew, was essential. If a doctor was going to do his best work, he needed to concentrate on his patients.

"How do you feel, Mr. Osborne?" he asked. Though it still felt a little odd, addressing someone younger than himself as "Mister," Dwight knew it was important. The formal title gave the patients dignity, and that was one of the few things he could offer to men who had suffered the indignities of war.

Though the other doctors disagreed and preferred to address their patients by their first names, Dwight wanted the young men to know that he respected them and their service. He wasn't like the blonde nurse who wouldn't stop flirting with them. Didn't she realize that she was treating them like schoolboys? They might be only eighteen or nineteen, but if they were old enough to fight, they were old enough to be afforded respect. Though thoughts of the blonde nurse irritated him, Dwight kept his face impassive. That was what a good doctor did.

"It hurts, Doc," the man said. "I feel like my leg's on fire."

With a heavy heart, Dwight uncovered what remained of the man's right leg, looking for signs of infection. How he had hated to amputate the leg, knowing that—even with a prosthesis—the young man would never live a totally normal life. He would walk, but he would never be able to run or play ball with his children. And, if the leg became infected, he might never walk. He might not even live long enough to return home. That was a prospect Dwight did not want to consider. Far too many men had died in this awful war that the politicians claimed would end all wars.

Dwight pulled aside the sterile gauze and studied the stump. Thank goodness, there were none of the angry red lines that he had feared! "It's healing well, Mr. Osborne," he said, keeping his voice even. There was no point in showing his elation, for that would reveal the fact that he had been concerned. A good doctor did not alarm his patients. A good doctor did not let his feelings show.

Dwight glanced out the window next to Private Osborne's bed. Today the wind no longer lashed the rain; instead, drops slid down the windows, partially obscuring the view of the moat. When he had first arrived in Goudot, Dwight had been surprised by the magnificence of the castle that had been converted to a base hospital. A three-story stone edifice with towers, turrets, and a moat was a far cry from a farmhouse in the Midwest and even further from the hospital of his dreams. Still, a man did what he had to.

"I can give you something more for the pain," he told Private Osborne. Wanting to alleviate pain was the reason Dwight had become a physician.

The young man shook his head. "I don't like that medicine. It makes me sleep." He looked down at his leg and frowned. "I'm afraid that I won't wake up."

"I understand." And Dwight did. Everyone feared something different. His youngest sister feared spiders; the oldest had a phobia about roaches; the nurses here feared him. All except the blonde one. She was different. It was distracting, the way she flirted with the patients, and that smile was enough to make a man forget what he was doing. Despite that, Dwight couldn't fault her competence. She was the best assistant he'd ever had.

He reached for the chart that hung at the foot of the hospital bed. "I'll have the nurse put extra salve on your leg when she dresses it. That should help."

The man nodded. As Dwight scribbled his orders on the chart, he heard a woman's footsteps, followed by a feminine voice. "Good afternoon, gentlemen." Though the voice sounded familiar, there was something odd about it, almost as if the speaker's nasal passages were congested. "How are things in Raindrop City today?"

Dwight started to smiled, then stopped himself. The staff seemed to have given everyone a nickname, and now it appeared that the town itself had one. It was an appropriate sobriquet. Not only did it rain here almost every day, but the word Goudot sounded like the French phrase *gouttes d'eau* or drops of water.

One of the men whistled. "Look at this, will you, boys? The sunshine just arrived."

The woman laughed. "Did I miss the sun? All I saw was mud—inches and inches of mud." The voice was definitely familiar, although the woman sounded as if she had a respiratory infection.

As Dwight started to pull the screen aside to see who would venture into a ward of seriously injured men with a potentially communicable disease, Private Osborne touched his arm. "Cover my leg, won't you, Doc? That way I can pretend . . ." There was no need for him to finish the sentence. If he couldn't see the missing limb, for a little while at least, he could pretend that the surgery had not taken place.

Dwight nodded. He shouldn't have let himself be distracted. The rustling on the other side of the screen told him the men were moving in their beds, probably getting ready for the nurse.

"You ready to write a letter for me?" one man asked.

The woman's voice was closer now, and Dwight could almost picture her walking from one bed to the next, checking on the patients. "Of course, Mr. Perkins. I'll be with you as soon as I finish the pans."

It was annoying that he couldn't place the voice. It was even more annoying that he cared. Resolutely, Dwight focused his attention on Private Osborne's chart.

"You know we don't like 'em any better than you do."

The men chuckled, and Dwight heard the clanking of metal as the woman emptied a bedpan. "Well, gentlemen, my granny says . . ."

Dwight almost dropped the chart. There was only one woman at this hospital who quoted her grandmother. He knew that. What he did not know was why she was here exposing wounded men to her respiratory infection. Dwight yanked the screen aside, intending to reprimand the blonde nurse. Instead he blinked, not quite believing what he saw. The pretty blonde nurse wasn't ill. She was wearing . . . No, it couldn't be.

"What is that contraption on your nose?" he demanded.

Those deep blue eyes that had smiled across an operating table widened ever so slightly. "It's called a clothespin."

"I can see that." Did the woman think he was stupid? Seven sisters generated a lot of laundry. As a result, Dwight had seen more clothespins than he cared to admit. Yet he had never seen a woman wearing one.

The nurse tipped her nose with the offending clothespin into the air. "If you knew that, why did you ask what it was?"

Impudent. She was worse than his sister Eve had been as a child. "Because," he said, sternly refusing to remember how he had laughed at Eve's antics, "for a moment I thought my eyes were deceiving me." This was, after all, a hospital, not a child's playroom. It was bad enough that this woman joked at inappropriate times. This was worse. "Would you kindly explain why you are wearing a clothespin?"

Dwight's eyes moved slowly from the top of her head to her feet, assessing the rest of her costume. The crisp white cap and apron were standard issue, as was the gray dress with its white collar and cuffs. It was only the clothespin that was out of place.

The nurse shrugged. "It makes my job easier." When she pointed toward the bedpan, a mischievous grin lighting her face, it was all Dwight could do not to laugh. Though he had more than a passing acquaintance with clothespins, having been pressed into laundry service on several occasions, he had never had to empty a bedpan. That was a situation he had no intention of changing. The nurse's solution to a known problem was ingenious and, yes, amusing. But a good doctor kept levity out of the hospital. A hospital was a serious place.

"A clothespin is not an authorized part of the uniform," Dwight informed the nurse. Didn't she understand the need for discipline? This wasn't simply a hospital; it was a hospital in a war zone. Regulations were not only needed, they were essential.

Apparently she did not understand, for she said simply, "I beg to disagree." Though her voice bore the soft twang Dwight associated with Texas, there was nothing soft about her attitude. Her head was held high, and despite the ridiculous item perched on her nose, she somehow appeared regal.

Dwight glared at the woman who was making a mockery of the hospital. "Kindly show me where the guidelines specify the use of a clothespin to block unpleasant odors."

The eyes that were bluer than a summer sky flashed with

annoyance. "Absence does not necessarily mean something is prohibited."

Dwight heard one of the patients muffle a sound. He chose not to listen too closely, for fear that he would identify the sound as a chuckle. This was not amusing! The woman's behavior was bordering on insubordination.

"What basis do you have for that statement?" he demanded.

"The handbook does not specifically authorize the wearing of spectacles, yet no one would stop a nurse from wearing them if she needed them."

This time there was no doubt about it. The men were laughing. "She's got you there, Doc," one announced.

"Nurse, I'd like to see you outside." He had to put a stop to this. If the nurses did not respect him, how could the patients trust him to help them? Dwight knew that more than medicine was required to heal a man, particularly a man who had been severely wounded. Sometimes faith was needed. Dwight's medical books had recounted numerous incidents where patients recovered when given a placebo, simply because they had confidence in the physician's abilities. He couldn't let anyone, especially not this flirtatious, distracting woman, endanger the patients by lessening their faith in him.

"C'mon, Doc," another patient said. "She wasn't hurting anyone. Truth is, we like Clothespin Carolyn." Carolyn. So that was her name. It suited her. Hadn't one of his sisters told him that the name meant "womanly"? Whatever else she was, there was no denying that this Carolyn was all woman.

"She makes us laugh," a third man chimed in.

Dwight knew when he was defeated. He would lose more than he could possibly gain if he continued this conversation with Clothespin Carolyn. "I'll bet she does." Picking up his bag, he walked toward the door. He would return to this ward when he was certain Carolyn and her clothespin were gone.

Thank goodness Louise wasn't like Carolyn. Louise wasn't flighty. She wasn't impudent. And Dwight couldn't imagine her even thinking about wearing a clothespin, much less actually doing it. Sensible, stable Louise was going to be the perfect doctor's wife. That was why he had asked her to marry him.

As he closed the door, Dwight heard one of the men say, "Don't take no notice of him, Carolyn. We like you."

It wasn't that he disliked Carolyn. Dwight couldn't argue with the fact that she had been efficient in the operating theater. He appreciated that. It was . . . Dwight stopped and shook his head as if to clear his thoughts. Why couldn't he define what he felt about Carolyn? He was a highly analytical man, known for the accuracy of his diagnoses. Why couldn't he identify the reason for his reaction to this woman? That wasn't like him. Not at all. It must be the weather. That was the only reason Dwight could imagine that his thoughts were scrambled.

"You should have seen him, Helen." Carolyn wielded the brush with a ferocity that had little relation to the amount of mud on her skirts. She had been dealing with mud-caked skirts and boots for days. Though she had groused about the rain and the inevitable mud, they had not irritated her the way a five-minute encounter with Dr. Hollow Heart had.

"At one point, I thought he was going to yank that clothespin off my nose," she continued. "Then I realized that Dwight . . . er, Dr. Hollins . . . would never display that much emotion."

Helen laughed as she measured tea and set the kettle to boil. The two women had returned to their room under the eaves. When Helen had seen Carolyn's agitation, she had prescribed a cup of tea, telling Carolyn it was the English panacea. "Now you know why we call him Hollow Heart," Helen said.

Indeed Carolyn did. She couldn't understand how Dwight . . . *Stop it*, she admonished herself. *He's Dr. Hollins or Dr. Hollow Heart, but not Dwight. There's no reason—absolutely no reason at all—to be thinking of him in such familiar terms.*

Carolyn laid down the brush and washed her hands. "Do you suppose anyone has ever seen him smile?" she asked Helen.

Helen unwrapped a piece of fruitcake that her mother had sent from home. Carolyn had been surprised when she learned that while it took weeks or even months for mail to arrive from the States, packages from London arrived within a day.

"I imagine Hollow Heart must have smiled at his fiancée once or twice," Helen said as she placed two slices of fruitcake on a plate. Though Carolyn's roommate had looked ill again this morning, now she glowed with health.

"Fiancée?" Carolyn could not camouflage her surprise. "Dw . . . er, Dr. Hollins is engaged?"

Helen shrugged. "So I've heard. The story is that her name is Louise and he gets a letter from her every Monday, regular as clockwork."

Rain continued to beat on the roof. When Helen had invited Carolyn to share the small room with her, she had explained that although they had more privacy here than in the nurses' quarters on the first and second floors, there was no escaping the sound of rain.

"It's hard to believe the man's human enough to love someone." Carolyn wondered if he looked at Louise with the same disdain that he'd shown her. Of course not. Louise was probably the type of woman who did exactly what he expected. She wouldn't wear a clothespin, and Carolyn doubted she'd ever defied him.

As she poured two cups of tea and handed one to Car-

olyn, Helen said, "You never know. People were surprised
when I fell in love with Glen. They always thought I'd
marry the boy next door. I might have, too," she said,
breaking a piece of fruitcake and chewing it carefully. "But
when I met Glen, I knew he was the one man for me. And
look at me now, an old married woman." Helen gave Carolyn an appraising glance. "Was it that way for you, too?"

Carolyn spooned sugar into her cup and took her time
stirring it while she tried to compose her reply. What
should she say? Everyone knew she was engaged. The ring
on her left hand was proof of that. The reasons, however,
were known only to her. Not even Ed understood why she
had accepted his offer of marriage. Though she had shared
many secrets with Ed over the years, that was one he would
never learn.

Carolyn settled on the truth, or at least part of it. "The
folks at home were surprised by my engagement, too," she
admitted. Surprise was a mild way to describe the total
disbelief that the announcement had created in Canela. "But
it was for the opposite reason. No one thought I'd marry
Ed, *because* he was the boy next door."

Helen's expression was thoughtful as she sipped her tea,
and Carolyn wondered if something she had said had told
Helen more than she'd intended. "Then it wasn't what the
French would call a *coup de foudre*?" Helen asked.

"A lightning bolt? Not really." Not at all. "Ed and I were
best friends all our lives. You could say that one thing led
to another." The war, her own impetuosity, Ed's fears.
They were all reasons she now wore a diamond on her left
hand. But Helen didn't need to know that. Nor did Ed.

Helen nodded as if satisfied. "Love is wonderful, no matter where you find it." She touched her wedding band.

"And it has many forms," Carolyn added. For she did
love Ed. He was her dearest friend. Agreeing to marry him
wasn't a mistake any more than coming to France had been.

That night Carolyn pulled out her stationery. Unlike

Dwight's Louise, she did not write to Ed only once a week. She tried to send him a note, even if only a brief one, every day or two, for she knew how important mail was to the soldiers in the trenches.

Dear Ed. Carolyn crumpled the paper and grabbed another piece. She would address a friend as "dear." Her fiancé deserved more. *Dearest Ed.* That was better. *I know you of all people won't be surprised by my latest adventure.* Growing up next door, he'd been aware of the scrapes that her impetuosity had gotten her into, and more than once he'd pretended that she had been with him, when the truth was she had been doing things that would have alarmed her parents, including attempting to drive the family's brand new automobile.

Yesterday I worked as a nurse in the operating room. Can you picture that? The girl who cried when you skinned your knees—and, thanks to the awkwardness that Ed had never outgrown, that had happened frequently—*was there, helping to dig out pieces of mortar and stitch—correction: 'suture'—wounds.* She wouldn't think about the amputation, and she certainly wouldn't tell a man on the front lines that another man would never again walk normally. Ed was all too aware of the dangers of battle.

Knowing my luck, you won't be surprised that I had to work with the most difficult doctor. To say it wasn't easy is an understatement, but we both survived the experience and, more importantly, we helped many wounded.

Be careful, dearest Ed. And when this war is over, we'll have a wedding Canela will remember for years.

Carolyn closed her eyes, picturing her wedding. She was walking down the aisle, dressed in her grandmother's gown, carrying a bouquet of white roses. There at the front of the church, her groom was waiting. He was tall, with medium brown hair and hazel eyes. Carolyn's eyes flew open. Why on earth was she conjuring the image of Dwight Hollins? It must be the weather that was confusing her thoughts so badly. That's all it could be. Ed, red-haired, green-eyed, freckled, lanky Ed Bleeker was the man she was going to marry.

Of course he was.

Chapter Three

Maybe if it would stop raining, he'd feel better. Dwight gave himself a mental shake as he walked through the mess line. He was supposed to be a brilliant diagnostician, able to examine a patient and quickly assess his problems. Even more importantly, he was reputed to be almost infallible in his determination of the correct treatment. Infallible, hah!

Dwight nodded as the elderly woman who stood behind the serving table, a perpetual frown on her face, offered him scrambled eggs. Though many of the delicacies which had made France a gastronomic wonderland were in short supply, the neighboring farms' chickens seemed unaffected by the artillery shelling. Thank heavens for small mercies. The weather might be miserable, but at least the food was edible. Even though the chefs who had once created culinary masterpieces for the chateau's inhabitants had fled, nothing could destroy the flavor of these eggs. Dwight wasn't sure what seasonings the new cooks used; all he knew was that the eggs in Goudot were superior to any he'd eaten at home on the farm, and that was saying a great deal.

He accepted the brioche the woman offered him, knowing it was futile to ask for toast. The light roll was the only breakfast bread available. Dwight frowned as he made his way to one of the smaller tables. The nurses normally ate at the long table in the middle of the room, and occasionally a doctor would join them. Dwight had done that once, but the awkward silence that had greeted him had told him he was being tolerated, not welcomed.

He frowned again. It wasn't the nurses, the absence of toast or even his patients that were bothering him this morning. The problem was himself. He, the brilliant diagnostician, could not explain it. His life was no different than it had been a week ago. Dwight knew that as surely as he knew that it had rained for seven of the last seven days. Nothing had changed, and yet he felt as if he had lost something important. The worst part was, he couldn't explain what it was that seemed to be missing. Something was making him stare out the window, looking for someone who never came. Something was making him waken in the middle of the night, listening for the sound that somehow eluded him. Something was wrong, and he hadn't an inkling what it might be.

He swallowed the eggs, washing them down with a cup of coffee, oblivious to the flavor that just a week ago had pleased him.

"Something wrong, Hollins?" One of the other doctors asked as he plunked his plate onto the table next to Dwight.

Dwight shook his head. "Nothing more than usual." It was a lie, but what was the point of admitting that you hadn't the slightest idea why you felt morose one moment and then ready to laugh with joy the next? It had to be the effect of the incessant rain.

"Heard from home?" The other doctor's attempts to make conversation were almost as incessant as the rain.

This time Dwight nodded. "I can always count on Louise." As he pronounced the words, Dwight's eyes widened. That was what was wrong. Louise's last letter had been shorter than usual. That was why he was feeling so out of sorts. Of course it was. It couldn't be anything else.

An hour later Dwight stared at the man on the gurney, assessing the extent of his injuries. Private Rogers was luckier than most. Though he had been exposed to poisonous gas, he was still alive. His biggest risk now was infection, caused by the weakened state of his lungs. Dwight scribbled a note on the man's chart, then turned to the next patient. Sergeant Scanlon was not so lucky. Shrapnel had torn a huge hole in his leg, shattering the fibia. It would take more than luck. It would take all the skill Dwight possessed to save this man's leg. Dwight felt the adrenaline rush through him as he accepted the challenge. He would save the leg. That was why he had become a doctor. That was why he had come to France.

"Scalpel," he called. Dwight's order was followed by the sound of metal clanging on the floor. He glared at the nurse. Didn't she understand what was at stake here? "Scalpel," he repeated. "And maybe this time you can place it in my hand." Her movements jerky, the nurse dropped the blade end of the scalpel onto his outstretched palm. Instinctively, Dwight recoiled, and the instrument tumbled to the floor without lacerating his hand. The adrenaline that had been preparing him for a difficult surgical process began to fade, replaced by anger.

"Nurse—what's your name?"

"Helen Guthrie." Her voice trembled almost as much as her hand had. It was infuriating, the way the nurses seemed to find even the most elementary tasks difficult.

Dwight fixed his stare on her. "Very well, Nurse Guthrie," he said, holding out his hand for a scalpel. "Are you aware that the reason you're here is to assist me?"

"Yes, Doctor."

"Then do so, and kindly refrain from causing lacerations. We have more than enough injuries to treat without our staff inflicting others."

Though she did not fumble again, Nurse Guthrie's movements were awkward, and the sidelong glances she gave him reminded Dwight of a frightened rabbit he had once seen cowering under a branch. Dwight tried not to sigh with frustration. The nurse was obviously afraid of him. They all were.

He knew they called him Hollow Heart and that they thought he had no emotions. They were wrong. He cared— oh, how he cared—about these patients. The soldiers were fighting in almost unbelievably primitive conditions, living in mud-filled trenches, sharing their quarters with rats whose size was legendary, somehow dealing with the incessant noise of artillery. When they were wounded, it was Dwight's responsibility to heal them. And to do that, he needed nurses. He didn't demand perfection, only competence. Was that so unreasonable? Apparently Nurse Guthrie thought it was.

Dwight clenched his jaw as he studied his patient's leg, knowing that his success depended in part on the woman who was assisting him. There had to be one nurse who wouldn't cower in his presence, one who could do her job. The other doctors claimed they had no such problems. That might be true, but those same doctors sent the most difficult injuries to Dwight. If he was going to save lives, he needed the best nurse Goudot had to offer, and that was not Nurse Guthrie.

As he tied the suture, Dwight heard a burst of laughter from the ward next door. The sound was so unexpected that it broke his concentration, and for a second he felt a flicker of annoyance. Then the realization hit him with the force of an ornery mule's kick. That was it! That was the answer to his problem!

Dwight glanced at the window. The day was still gray and somber. Rain still lashed against the panes. Nothing had changed, and yet he couldn't ignore the way he felt, as if he had found the elusive something he'd been seeking for the past week.

"Miss Pierce." As soon as surgery was over, Dwight made his way to the head nurse's tiny office. Now that he knew what he needed, he would waste no time in obtaining it.

"How may I assist you, Dr. Hollins?" If the gray-haired head of nurses was surprised by his appearance, she gave no sign of it. Nor, he noted with approval, did her hands tremble. Perhaps there were two members of the nursing staff who weren't afraid of him.

"My request is fairly simple," he said. "I need you to ensure that Carolyn . . ." Dwight shrugged his shoulders. "I don't know her last name," he admitted, "but the patients call her Clothespin Carolyn." To Miss Pierce's credit, she did not react to the sobriquet. "I need Carolyn to serve as my operating room assistant henceforth."

The nurse shook her head. "I'm sorry, Doctor, but I can't do that."

It was not the response Dwight had expected, and it most definitely was not the one he wanted. "Has that particular nurse left our hospital?" That was the only reason he could imagine for the refusal.

"Oh, no, Doctor, she has not. But . . ."

Thank goodness! Dwight tried to ignore the rush of satisfaction that surged through him when he realized that it was indeed Carolyn who had caused the patients' laughter. "If she's here, I see no reason why she cannot be assigned to me."

"There is a reason, I assure you." Miss Pierce pursed her lips, as if annoyed by Dwight's persistence. Didn't she understand that men's lives were at stake? Dwight needed Clothespin Carolyn, and not because she was the most beautiful woman he'd ever seen. Beauty had nothing to do with his request.

"Pray, tell me why I cannot have the one nurse who possesses more than a modicum of competence."

The head nurse folded her hands on her desk, giving Dwight the impression she was praying for patience. So was he. This whole conversation was absurd. A doctor shouldn't have to plead for the right equipment or the right assistant.

"You've just identified the problem, Dr. Hollins. Carolyn Wentworth is not a nurse; she's an aide."

"Impossible! She assisted me the other day."

Miss Pierce regarded Dwight as if he were slightly demented. "You must be mistaken," she said, her voice low and filled with concern. "Miss Wentworth is not trained as a nurse. There is no reason she would have been in the operating room."

"She was there," Dwight said coldly. He was not accustomed to having his word questioned, especially on something this important. "Might I suggest that we ask her to explain what happened."

"Certainly, Doctor."

It must be the weather. That was the only explanation Carolyn could find for the way she felt. Nothing else made any sense. She sat on the edge of her bed and eased off her shoes. Her feet always ached at the end of a shift in the wards. But aching feet were not what bothered her. The emptiness was. She couldn't understand it. The patients appreciated her; and she knew that she was helping them, if only in a small way. That should have filled her with satisfaction, and yet—for some reason—she felt as if something important was missing from her life. Carolyn might have called it homesickness, but she knew it wasn't that. Though she missed her sisters and her life in Canela, this was a different feeling, a hollowness deep inside her. It must be caused by the incessant rain. It couldn't be anything else.

The door flew open. "There you are." Helen's face was red with exertion, and the way she was panting told Carolyn she had run up the stairs. "Miss Pierce wants to see you. She looks angry."

Carolyn slid her feet back into her shoes. A summons from the head nurse was not to be ignored. "Do you suppose she heard about the clothespin?" Dwight, that is Doctor Hollins, had seemed to believe that was a major infraction. Had he reported it to Miss Pierce?

"I don't think that would bother her." Though the worried look on Helen's face told Carolyn how unusual it was for Miss Pierce to be angry, her roommate put a reassuring hand on her shoulder. "Do you want me to go with you?"

Carolyn shook her head. "Whatever it is, I need to face her alone."

But when Carolyn entered Miss Pierce's office, she discovered that the head nurse was not alone. The gray-haired woman who had been so kind to her on her first day in Goudot sat behind her desk, her hands folded in front of her. On the opposite side of the desk, his back to the door, sat the man whose image had disturbed far too many of Carolyn's dreams. She felt her heart skip a beat. That was surely caused by apprehension over what Miss Pierce would say, not by the sight of the head nurse's visitor. There was no reason he or any man other than Ed should make her heart race.

Dwight Hollins rose to his feet and inclined his head in a gesture that Carolyn could only describe as regal. His expression was impassive, confirming her belief that the man would never show emotion.

"I would like you to clarify something for us," Miss Pierce said, her voice laced with asperity. She gave Carolyn an assessing look that made her feel she was under a roentgen machine and that Miss Pierce was examining not only her bones but her very thoughts. It was a decidedly uncomfortable feeling.

The head nurse raised one eyebrow. "Dr. Hollins believes that you assisted him in surgery several days ago. I assured him that he was mistaken, but he would like to hear that from you."

Carolyn turned toward the doctor. This was worse than the clothespin. No wonder Miss Pierce was angry. Carolyn's charade had been uncovered, and she would be sent home in disgrace. Though she was tempted to lie, the realization that that was the act of a coward stopped her. Whatever else she was, Carolyn was not a coward. She might be impulsive; people might consider her flighty. She wouldn't deny either accusation, but she was neither a liar nor a coward.

"Dr. Hollins is not mistaken," she said firmly. Though her words were directed to the head nurse, Carolyn kept her eyes fixed on the doctor. He had gotten her into this predicament. She wanted to see his reaction. Undoubtedly he would laugh at her discomfiture.

It happened so quickly that Carolyn thought she might have been the one who was mistaken, but when the action was repeated, she knew her eyes had not deceived her. Dwight's lips had started to twitch, as if he were tempted to smile. How dare he gloat at her?

It was Miss Pierce who spoke. "How is that possible?" she demanded, her voice frosty. "I did not assign you to the operating room."

This time Carolyn turned to the nurse. "No, you did not," she agreed. "One of the nurses was too ill to work." Deliberately Carolyn did not mention Helen's name. There was nothing to be gained by involving her friend. "That day we had an unusually high number of wounded. Since there was no one else to help Dr. Hollins, I did what I could."

As she spoke, Carolyn saw the color rise in the other woman's cheeks. If Miss Pierce had been angry before, she was furious now. Her face was almost as red as the Red Cross insignia she wore on her cap and left arm.

"I'm sorry, Dr. Hollins," Miss Pierce said, her hands clenched as she rose from behind her desk. "I can promise you that this will never happen again."

Carolyn darted a glance at the doctor, expecting to see him gloating. This must be his way of repaying her for the clothespin episode. Instead, he gave her a look that appeared to be almost conspiratorial. That wasn't possible, of course. Dwight Hollins had no reason to be conspiring with her.

"To the contrary," he said, fixing his gaze on Miss Pierce, "I expect it to happen regularly. I expect Miss Wentworth to assist me whenever I'm in the operating room. Find someone else to take over her other duties. I need her."

"But, Doctor," Miss Pierce protested, her voice seething with anger. "This is highly irregular."

It wasn't Carolyn's imagination. She was sure it wasn't a figment that the room crackled with tension and that Miss Pierce was regarding Dwight Hollins with barely controlled hostility. In all likelihood, this was the first time anyone had challenged the head nurse's authority.

Dwight nodded ever so slightly, as if acknowledging the truth of Miss Pierce's words. "Perhaps my request is irregular, but so, too, is war. Now, unless Miss Wentworth would prefer to empty bedpans, I see no reason that she should not serve as my assistant."

Though the color in the head nurse's cheeks remained high, her voice was once more gentle when she addressed Carolyn. "The choice is yours, Carolyn. If you're going to work in the operating room, I'll see to it that you are given additional training. The question is, do you want to assist Dr. Hollins?"

It was clear that Miss Pierce expected a negative response. Carolyn shifted her gaze to the doctor. He stood there, waiting for her decision. She ought to refuse, if only to show the man that not everyone would bend to his will.

But the memory of his saying "I need her" was too fresh. This was why Carolyn had come to France—to be useful.

"I'll do it," she said.

Miss Pierce's lips thinned. "Very well, Doctor. You've gotten your way . . . again. Come with me, Carolyn."

When she returned to their room and told Helen what had happened, her roommate was incredulous. "I can't believe that you agreed!" Helen lit the gas ring and set the kettle on it. When she had adjusted the flame, she turned back to Carolyn. "There's not a single nurse who would willingly work for that man. All he does is complain about us and tell us we're incompetent." Helen spooned tea into the pot, then gave Carolyn an appraising look. "What did you do differently from us?"

It was the question Carolyn had asked herself countless times as Miss Pierce tutored her on operating room protocol. What had she done that the real nurses had not?

"I have no idea. If anything, I would have said that I irritated him." Carolyn remembered how the doctor had glowered when she curtseyed to the patients and how his frown had deepened each time she had smiled. "I don't know why he thinks I can help him." Carolyn unpinned her cap and ran her fingers through her hair, grateful that she had a short bob like the famous dancer Irene Castle. Long hair like Helen's was more difficult to care for, especially in the rain. "I hated surgery," Carolyn continued. "Dr. Hollins had to have realized that."

"That assumes that the man paid any attention to what you were feeling." Helen took a step toward Carolyn. "If you hated surgery that much, why did you agree?"

The answer was simple. "To help the men. How could I possibly say no?" If Theo and Ed could fight to make the world safe for democracy, Carolyn could do her best to save the lives of those who were wounded.

A smile quirked Helen's lips. "I could say no to working

with Hollow Heart. The man makes me so nervous that I forget everything I learned in nursing school."

Carolyn shrugged. "He doesn't make me nervous; he just irritates me." Carolyn thought of the look he'd given her when she hadn't recognized a scalpel and how that condescending expression had spurred her. "This may sound peculiar, but somehow he makes me determined to prove that I'm competent." She reached for her clothes brush. Though she couldn't sweep away the memory of how the doctor had wanted to laugh at her discomfort in Miss Pierce's office, she could brush the mud from her skirts. "Dwight Hollins is without a doubt the most annoying man I've ever met." The words came out more forcefully than she had intended.

Helen blinked, then gave Carolyn a long look. "I wonder if . . ." Her eyes fell to Carolyn's left hand and the diamond that sparkled on her ring finger. "No," she said, shaking her head. "It's too far-fetched."

"What are you talking about?"

"Nothing. Nothing at all." But Helen's words were not convincing.

Chapter Four

"Good afternoon, gentlemen." Though she kept what she hoped looked like a carefree smile fixed on her face, Carolyn scanned the room, trying to judge the patients' mood. When she had visited them two days earlier, they had seemed cheerful. Today, despite the rays of sunshine that lit the room, there was a palpable gloom. The reason, Carolyn guessed, was the empty bed by the window. The damage to Private Rogers' lungs had proven too great, and she had heard that he had succumbed to infection last night. That was one of the reasons she had come to the ward today, even though she was exhausted from her time in the operating room. It was physically tiring, standing for so many hours. But that fatigue was nothing compared to the emotional drain of trying to save critically wounded men.

"How are you on this beautiful day?" Carolyn asked, gesturing toward the window. Thank goodness the sun had finally appeared. After days of seemingly endless rain, the sunny interlude was a welcome change. Though nothing could compensate for the loss of a comrade, the absence of rain had to boost the men's spirits, even if only slightly.

"We're just peachy," one of the men said, his dour tone belying the lighthearted words.

37

"I reckon we'd be a darn sight better if we were home," the redheaded man in the next bed told her.

Carolyn nodded. They would all be a darn sight better— to use the corporal's expression—if the war were over and they were home. "Well, gentlemen," she said, continuing the fable she had begun a week ago, "you know that I commissioned the SS Carolyn to take us all back to the States. Unfortunately, this morning's carrier pigeon told me that there was a delay at the shipyard, and it'll be at least another month before the boat is ready. In the meantime . . ."

"Are you gonna read to us?" the dour-voiced man asked.

Carolyn shook her head and reached for the canvas bag she'd brought with her. "I figured you were tired of my voice." *Besides,* she added silently, *you need something different to take your mind off the empty bed.* "I propose to beat you gentlemen at Parcheesi," she announced. Suiting her actions to her words, she pulled a small table from between two of the beds and spread the game board on it.

When she had been packing her trunk and had reached for the game, Martha had raised her eyebrows in surprise.

"Why do you want that?" her sister had asked.

Carolyn hadn't been able to explain the impulse. All she knew was that she wanted the game that had helped while away rainy days for the four Wentworth children. She hadn't taken it from her trunk until today when she had heard about Private Rogers.

"Parcheesi. I ain't played that since I was a boy," the redhead told her.

"Me, neither," said the man in the next bed.

Carolyn grinned. "All the better for me." She placed the counters at the edges of the board and plunked a pair of dice in the center. "If you're out of practice, I'll have a better chance of winning." Carolyn remembered the times she'd begged for just one more game, in the hope that she'd win that one. No matter how many rematches she demanded, Theo remained the undisputed Parcheesi champion of the Wentworth family. "I feel it only fair to warn you that I don't like to lose," she told the patients. "Now, who's willing to take on Champ Carolyn?"

"Count me in." A sparkle of animation lit the somber man's face, and for the first time since she had entered the room, his voice had lost its bitter tone.

"I reckon, even if it is a child's game, it's better than nothin'," the redhead said as he reached for a counter.

When Carolyn had coaxed a third man into joining them, she turned to the redhead. "It's not simply a child's game," she said in her best schoolmarm tone. "I read that couples used to take Parcheesi boards on their honeymoons."

A hoot of laughter greeted her announcement. "Is that what you're fixing to do?" one of the men asked.

Carolyn shook her head in mock solemnity. "My granny said it was bad luck to discuss a girl's honeymoon with anyone other than her intended." The truth was, her normally vivid imagination had trouble picturing herself on a honeymoon with Ed, with or without a Parcheesi board.

"What did your granny say about people who cheated?"

"Who would do a thing like that?"

The man stared at one corner of the board. As Carolyn followed the direction of his gaze, she saw that the redhead's counter had moved, though it was not yet his turn. "Why, Granny would call him a lazy, no-count rapscallion," she said calmly.

The first man nodded and fixed his gaze on the redhead. "All right, you lazy, no-count rapscallion, put that counter back where it belongs."

"Aw, shucks." The redhead frowned. "If I don't cheat, I reckon I won't win the prize."

"What prize?" Carolyn hadn't expected the men to demand a prize. She thought quickly. If they insisted, she'd give them an autographed clothespin.

The redhead shrugged. "I figured you was gonna give the winner a kiss." He stared at her lips.

Carolyn tried not to laugh at the man's earnest expression. Several of the nurse's aide training sessions had stressed how much the men craved female companionship and that they saw the aides as substitutes for their mothers, sisters, wives, and fiancées. Cases of patients imagining themselves in love with a nurse or an aide were common, the instructor had said. Carolyn knew she should have anticipated that possibility and done whatever she could to discourage the men as gently as possible. Next time she would come prepared with prizes to forestall such requests. That was next time. There was still today to handle.

Dabbing at her eyes, as if she were on the verge of weeping, she said, "I hate to disappoint y'all, but I'm afraid a kiss is one thing I can't offer you. My granny told me that a girl must never kiss anyone other than her husband."

"Shucks!"

The first man laughed. "It appears to me that that grandmother of yours was a mighty wise woman, Nurse Carolyn."

"That's what she always told me."

The men laughed, all except the one who had entered the room, unseen by the Parcheesi players. Carolyn wasn't certain how he did it, but Dwight Hollins managed to frown at the same time that he raised an eyebrow.

"I'm surprised to see you, Miss Wentworth," he said in the frosty tones she knew so well. "I thought you had been relieved of ward duty."

Carolyn shrugged, then gave the men a quick smile. "I'm here as a friend, not an aide," she explained.

The redhead chuckled. "That's why she ain't wearing her clothespin."

"I see." Though Dwight nodded as if he understood, Carolyn doubted he did. The man was so solemn, she wondered if he did anything for pure enjoyment. The patients might think she came to the wards for their benefit, but the one who truly benefited from the visits was Carolyn herself. She enjoyed both the men's camaraderie and the thought that she was helping them. Those things brought her pleasure. She wasn't certain anything brought Dwight Hollins pleasure.

"If you're free, Miss Wentworth," he said, "I wondered if you would like to accompany me on my rounds. It seems only fair that you have a chance to see the progress our patients have made."

For a second, Carolyn's jaw dropped in surprise. "Our" patients? Though it was true she had thought of them in those terms, it had never occurred to her that Dwight considered her anything more than an extension of him in the operating room.

"Certainly, Doctor," she said. After a quick goodbye to the men, she gathered her cloak and joined Dwight. As they crossed the courtyard that separated the two hospital wards, she looked at the man who walked next to her. Perhaps it was the result of the sunshine, an undeniable boost to the spirits. Perhaps it was something else. Carolyn wasn't sure why, but it seemed that he was more relaxed today than she'd ever seen him.

"Have you always wanted to be a doctor?" she asked. Though he might freeze her with another one of those stares that the nurses dreaded, telling her wordlessly that she had overstepped the bounds, Carolyn had decided to risk his censure. The man was a puzzle, and she had always enjoyed solving puzzles.

"Almost." Dwight's hazel eyes shone with an enthusiasm that was not reflected in his voice. "I was seven the day I knew I was going to be a doctor."

Carolyn noted that he had said "going to be" rather than "wanted to be." It appeared that even at that age, he had been a determined boy. "What happened?" she asked. Though his voice had been emotionless, Carolyn realized that something dramatic must have occurred to make the young Dwight so certain of his future. At seven, she had dreamed of nothing more ambitious than getting married. She certainly hadn't envisioned being in France, helping save soldiers' lives.

Dwight stopped and looked down at her. This time his eyes were somber. "My youngest sister fell out of the hayloft. For a minute, I thought she was dead." While Dwight continued to speak in his normal, calm tones, Carolyn shuddered as she pictured the scene in the barn. "When I realized Eve was alive but barely breathing, I knew there was only one thing to do. I hitched the mule to the wagon and drove her into town to the doctor." A faint smile crossed Dwight's face. Like the one she had seen in Miss Pierce's office, it was fleeting, almost as if Dwight's lips had forgotten how to smile.

"At the end of the day, I had a hero," he told her. "It wasn't just that Doc Sherman saved my sister's life. He let me help him when he performed the tracheotomy. After that, there was only one thing I wanted to do with my life."

Carolyn stared, not sure what amazed her more: the fact that the doctor had allowed a child to assist him or that a child would want to be part of so dangerous an operation. "You were seven!"

Dwight's smile broadened and for a second Carolyn was speechless. Dwight Hollins could smile—and, oh, what a smile! In repose, he was a handsome man, but with his face softened by a smile, he could easily star in a Hollywood film.

"Why do you find that hard to believe?"

Carolyn had a moment of confusion. Surely she hadn't voiced her thought that he looked like a movie star.

As Dwight continued, she remembered what she had said before his smile had distracted her. "Most of us were seven once."

But very few of us would have reacted positively to

watching a doctor cut a hole in our sister's throat. Carolyn was careful not to say that. Instead, she replied, "Most of us aren't so sure of our vocation then."

Dwight shrugged and looked around the courtyard, as if he were seeing it for the first time. The chateau was constructed as a square with the four wings surrounding a central courtyard, a single large gate providing access to it. In earlier times, formal gardens had edged the open space, but the war had changed that, and now there was only mud.

Though the courtyard was bleak, nothing could destroy the beauty of the building itself. Constructed of gray stone with a darker gray slate roof, it was perfectly proportioned, the courtyard large enough that the three-story castle did not overwhelm it.

Carolyn glanced up at the window of the room she shared with Helen. Like all the rooms on the top floor, the window was a dormer set into the steeply pitched roof. Carolyn had seen dormers before, but the ones at home had been utilitarian. They had not been topped with beautiful stone carvings. And none of the buildings she had ever seen in Texas had boasted towers that made them look like a castle from one of the fairytales her mother had read to Carolyn and her sisters.

When she was seven, she had listened to fairytales. The man who stood so close to her had chosen his life's work at the same age. Carolyn looked at Dwight, trying to picture him as a seven-year-old. "I imagine your family was proud of you."

To her surprise, Dwight shook his head. "Dad wanted me to be a farmer like him; Mother just wanted whatever Dad did. I knew I'd have to convince them that this was right for me."

Again, she was amazed. Dwight was unlike anyone she'd ever met. "Obviously, you did convince your parents."

As Dwight shrugged, the sun glinted off one of the brass buttons on his uniform. "Not right away. At first they figured I'd grow out of it. When I didn't and it was clear that they weren't going to approve, I changed my tactics." Dwight gestured toward the corner of the chateau that was reserved for officers. "No general planned his strategy more carefully than I did." It wasn't a boast, merely a simple statement of fact. "The first thing I did was convince Doc Sherman to let me help him."

"And your parents agreed to that?" It didn't sound likely, given the way Dwight had described them.

"Not really. They told me I could go into town when I finished my work on the farm. Then they gave me more chores to do."

"Yet somehow you managed to finish them."

Two of the nurses left their wing. When they saw Carolyn and Dwight, though they nodded a greeting, Carolyn noticed that they walked along the perimeter of the courtyard rather than taking the direct route that would have brought them close to Dwight.

Seeming oblivious to the nurses' shunning, Dwight continued his explanation. "I enlisted my sisters' help. To put it bluntly, I bribed them. I used the money I earned working for the doctor to buy my sisters ribbons and lace and the other things seven young girls craved."

"Seven? You have seven sisters?" There were days when Carolyn thought two were too many.

"Yes, indeed." Dwight seemed faintly amused by Carolyn's reaction. "I'm the oldest child and the only male."

The elder Mr. Hollins' behavior suddenly made sense. "No wonder your father wanted you to be a farmer. He wants to leave the farm to you."

Twin furrows appeared between Dwight's eyes as he considered Carolyn's words. "I never thought of that."

Carolyn knew all about dynasties and inheritances, but perhaps that was because she had lived in a town rather than on a farm. "My father took Theo to the bank from the time he was ten."

"Theo, I gather, is your brother."

Carolyn nodded, bemused. Who would have thought that her casual question would have resulted in her standing here in the courtyard trading family histories with Dwight Hollins? "I'm from a smaller family than you," she told him. "Martha's two years older than me. The twins—that's Theo and Emily—are two years younger."

"So you're in the middle." Dwight's expression was pensive. "I sometimes wondered what it would be like to be a middle child."

And Carolyn had wondered what it would have been like if she'd been the oldest. "Most of the time I felt as if I had two mothers, my real one and Martha." Carolyn remembered all the advice Martha had given her and how vehemently her older sister had protested when she had announced her intention of becoming a nurse's aide. "Didn't you take care of your sisters?"

"I suppose I did, when there was time. Looking back, though, it seems like I spent every waking moment preparing to be a doctor."

It was odd. When he'd invited her to accompany him on his rounds, Dwight had seemed in a hurry. Now he was apparently content to stand in the sunshine, talking. "You must have had some time off," she said. "After all, you fell in love."

For a second, Dwight's expression was blank, as if he did not understand her words. Then he nodded brusquely. "Oh, yes. Of course. Louise. A doctor needs a wife like Louise."

Carolyn stared at him. Dwight sounded the way he had when he had explained his tactics for gaining his parents' acceptance. It was one thing to plan your education, quite another to choose a wife according to plan. "You sound as if you had a schedule. Step one, finish medical school; step two, find a wife." Carolyn could picture him making a list the way she did when she was going shopping.

"Would it be so wrong if I had?" Dwight glanced down at her left hand. "Surely you and . . ." He paused, obviously searching for her fiancé's name.

"Ed."

"You and Ed must have planned the best time to become engaged."

"Actually, we didn't. It just happened."

It had been late summer, one of those days when the sun shone from a sky so deeply blue that it almost hurt her eyes. Though the thermometer declared that it was close to a hundred, a light breeze and the shade of the live oak would have made it pleasant to sit on the swing, gliding ever so slowly, if the situation had not been so serious. Today was the day she and her sisters had dreaded. Not waiting to be drafted, Theo had enlisted in the Army.

"What will I do if he's killed?" Carolyn turned to the young man sitting next to her. When Martha and Emily had asked the same question, she had shook her head vehemently, denying that it could happen. Although Carolyn knew the realities of war and the heavy casualties the Allies had already endured, someone needed to be strong. Someone needed to hold out hope. But now that she was with Ed, there was no need for pretense. He would understand. "I can't bear the thought of a world without Theo," Carolyn said, her voice cracking with emotion.

She had expected Ed to murmur soothing words. Instead, he took her hand between both of his and turned until he was facing her. "I wish someone cared whether or not I came back," he said, his voice as bleak as her sisters' had been when they spoke of Theo's enlistment.

"What do you mean?" Never before had Carolyn seen Ed so serious.

"I enlisted this morning."

Carolyn felt the blood drain from her face. "Oh, Ed! Why did you do that?" Though everything else was changing around her, she had somehow believed that Ed would remain at home, that the draft would not take him. And now he had enlisted!

The expression in his green eyes was almost reproachful as he said, "The same reason Theo did. I want to serve my country. Besides," Ed lowered his eyes, as if he were ashamed of what he was about to say. "I figured I was expendable. No one would miss me."

Carolyn's heart ached at the thought that Ed would believe that. "Don't be ridiculous!" She squeezed his hand. "We'd all miss you. Your parents would miss you. I'd miss you."

Ed managed a weak smile. "Sure you'd miss your pal—for a couple weeks." Beneath its thick coating of freckles, his face was pale, and Carolyn could feel his anguish. Poor Ed! He'd always been the odd one, tall, lanky, uncoordinated. When the other boys played sports, Ed was never asked to join them, for it was well known that he'd fumble the ball or trip over his feet. Though when he was with her, he could talk for hours, he was tongue-tied around other girls and—despite her coaxing—had never so much as asked one for a date. And now Ed, the boy who'd been her best friend, was going to war, thinking no one cared. She couldn't let him believe that.

"That's not true!" Carolyn said, her voice thick with emotion. "I want you to be safe. I love you, Ed." The words tumbled out, unplanned, but when she saw the spark of hope that lit Ed's eyes, she couldn't regret them.

"You don't really love me." This was the Ed she knew, convinced that no one could love him. "You're my friend."

"Of course I'm your friend." The droop of his mouth told Carolyn those were not the words he wanted to hear. She couldn't—she simply couldn't—let him go to war, thinking he had no reason to return. In another of those impetuous acts that her mother had warned her about, Carolyn laid her free hand on Ed's cheek, turning his face so that he was looking directly at her. She smiled, then low-

ered her eyes for a second. When she met his gaze again, she said softly, "I know it's forward of me to say this, but . . . well . . ." She ducked her head again. "If you were to ask me a certain question . . ." Carolyn let her voice trail off.

Ed gripped her hand so tightly it hurt. "Are you saying what I think you are?"

She smiled again. "Try asking me."

Though she would have thought it impossible, Ed's face paled even more, making his freckles more pronounced. He swallowed, cleared his throat, then swallowed again. For a second, she thought he was going to remain silent. Then he stammered, "Will you . . . er . . . will you marry me?"

She nodded. "Yes, Ed. I will." If Carolyn had had any doubts about the wisdom of her decision, the joy she saw on Ed's face erased them. She faced her family's protests and the town's incredulity calmly, refusing to explain what they all considered to be an inexplicable action, saying only that the war helped people see clearly what was important. For Carolyn, keeping Ed alive was the most important thing she could do.

"You mean you agreed to get married on a whim?" For an instant Carolyn stared at Dwight, startled by his words. She'd been so lost in her memories that for a few seconds she had been transported back to Texas in August.

She shook her head at the man who stood opposite her, his feet planted firmly on French ground, his brown hair gleaming in the October sun. "I didn't say that it was a whim." She would tell no one the reason for her engagement. "I love Ed. It's just that the war hastened our plans." Not wanting to discuss her own engagement any longer, she turned the tables. "Haven't you ever done anything spontaneously?"

Dwight shook his head. "I believe in thinking before I act."

"General Pershing could take lessons from you. Maybe you should command the American forces."

"Don't be ridiculous." This time there was nothing joking in Dwight's voice. "I want to save lives, not take them. That's what's important."

Carolyn couldn't dispute the importance of saving lives, but it wasn't everything. "What about fun? Where does that fit into your life plan?"

"It doesn't."

"But . . ." Carolyn started to protest. Dwight was wrong, so very wrong. For a second, she was tempted to tell him that and show him how to have fun. One look at his face quenched that thought. He wouldn't appreciate anyone telling him to laugh. This was Dwight Hollins, the man whose solemnity was legendary, the one who apparently planned every aspect of his life. Carolyn would take a lesson from him. She might not be able to plan her life, but in the future she would think before she spoke, especially when she was speaking to Dwight Hollins.

Dwight stared at the empty sheet of paper and frowned. It was getting late, and he still hadn't started his letter to Louise. He could blame it on the heavy workload, but the fact was, today had been no worse than any others. There was no reason why he had spent the last half hour sitting in the small room he shared with three other doctors, staring out the window rather than write a letter to Louise.

When he had left the States, he and Louise had agreed that they would write weekly, always on the same day. That way there would never be any question about when they should write. It had been such a good plan.

Dwight's lips curved in a smile at the memory of Carolyn's expression when she had spoken of spontaneity. It was obvious that he and she had very little in common. What would she think if she heard how he and Louise scheduled their correspondence? Carolyn would undoubtedly have some kind of sarcastic retort, probably telling him that women preferred spontaneity. She was wrong, of course. All women weren't like her. Louise most certainly was not.

Leaning back in his chair, Dwight closed his eyes, trying to picture the woman who would become his wife when the war ended. She was tall, slender, dark-haired—almost the complete opposite of Carolyn, who was medium height, nicely curved and blond. Dwight's eyes flew open and he frowned in disgust. Drat it all! Why did he keep thinking of Carolyn? It was Louise's smile he should be remembering, Louise's pretty face he should dream of. There was no reason he should think of Carolyn.

Dwight rose and began to pace the floor, trying to diagnose the cause of his errant thoughts. It had to be because Carolyn was here, and Louise was thousands of miles away. Pure proximity. Nothing else.

Dwight smiled in satisfaction. He was a good diagnostician. Now that he'd identified the cause of the problem, he knew how to cure it. *Think of Louise*, he admonished himself. She was the woman he was going to marry.

Dwight stared out the window, thankful that his room did not face the courtyard. He could see trees from here, and although they did not look like the trees at home, they were preferable to the sight of a muddy courtyard. Of course, he hadn't noticed the mud when he had been with Carolyn. It was only later when he had tried to clean his boots that he had realized he'd stood in inch-deep mud for close to half an hour.

Think of Louise. She wouldn't have stood in the mud. Louise was far too sensible for that. The truth was, that practicality was one of the things that had attracted Dwight. He had met Louise at one of the few social events he'd attended while he was a resident. She was beautiful and charming, but—more than that—he had realized she would be the perfect wife. The daughter of a doctor, Louise understood the demands of a physician's life. Just as important, she was a careful planner like Dwight himself. *Spontaneity* was not a word in her vocabulary, any more than it was in his.

Louise had developed a blueprint for her life, and that blueprint included marrying the right man, having three children, a home with a garden, and a cocker spaniel. She had already chosen the names for their children—three boys' and three girls' names, so they'd be prepared—and had begun looking for the perfect lot for their home. She had also started visiting dog breeders. "You can't start too early," she had told Dwight.

He, unfortunately, had not started early enough if he was going to finish his letter tonight. Dwight picked up the pen and began to write. *Dear Louise.* But though he told himself he needed to write, his mind refused to concentrate on the letter. Instead, he remembered the day they had become engaged. It had been Christmas, for Louise had said she had always dreamed of a Christmas engagement and a Midsummer Night's wedding. How her face had lit with pleasure when he had slipped the diamond ring onto her finger! It was silly to think that she'd been happier about the ring itself than about the prospect of marrying him. It was simply that the ring was new and she was the first of her friends to become engaged. That was the only reason Louise had spent the day visiting friends, showing off the diamond, while he'd remained at home celebrating the holiday with her family.

Dwight pushed that thought aside and began to write. He would tell Louise about the break in the rain and the hope of a Christmas truce. Those were safe topics. He would definitely not tell Louise about Carolyn and their discussion of engagements.

Dwight laid the pen on the desk and leaned back again, thinking. There was something mysterious about Carolyn's engagement. Or was there? Perhaps it was simply that it was different. It was clear that Carolyn's engagement bore little resemblance to his and that her agreement to marry Ed had been impulsive. And yet, who was to say that that was wrong? She loved Ed. She had said that. And he . . . Dwight frowned. He loved Louise; of course he did.

Carolyn poured herself a cup of tea and settled back in the one comfortable chair that the room boasted. The letter from Ed that had arrived that morning was on the table next to her, waiting to be read. But first she wanted to unwind, to put the day's events behind her.

Why had she gotten herself into such a predicament, discussing engagements? It wasn't as if she could blame anyone else. She was the one who'd introduced the subject. She should have realized that Dwight would turn the tables on her and ask her about Ed. But, no. No matter how many times her mother or Martha chided her for her impetuosity, she hadn't learned. She still spoke without thinking first.

Fortunately, Carolyn hadn't had to tell any lies to get out of the hole she'd dug. She simply hadn't told Dwight the entire truth. She had no intention of telling him—or anyone—that she had practically proposed to Ed and that she viewed her engagement as part of the war effort. She loved Ed. That was true. It was also true that she loved him as a friend or a brother, not as the man she was planning to marry. But that was one of those truths that she would not reveal. Not now. Probably not ever.

Carefully, she slit the envelope and pulled out the thin sheet of paper.

My darling Carolyn. Ed's handwriting was like him, big loopy letters that scrawled across the page. She smiled, remembering the notes they'd left in the crotch of the oak tree when they were children. Those letters had not started, "My darling."

Your letters mean more than I can ever tell you, he wrote. *The one thing the Army didn't prepare us for was boredom, and that's what we've got. Each day seems like the one before. We have Stand To at dawn. That's one of the two times a day that we get out of the trenches. You can't imagine how good it feels to stand on the ground with air—not dirt walls—around you. I've been told that the sunrise here in France is beautiful, but I can't vouch for it, since every day, every single day, it has rained at dawn.*

Once we eat (and I won't bore you with the litany of canned rations), it's time to tend to the donks. Carolyn smiled again. The first week, Ed had complained that the soldiers gave everything nicknames. Mules were called donkeys, or donks for short. Now, she noted, he'd adopted the abbreviation. *Mine kicked mud everywhere—all over me. Not that I was clean before then. Once Donk was fed, it was back into the trenches with nothing to do except wait for dusk and another Stand To.*

But then we had mail call. Carolyn, my dearest, your letter was better than sunshine. I tried to picture you with a clothespin on your nose, and that made me laugh for the first time in days. Thank you, my darling.

Carolyn squeezed her eyes closed to keep the tears from falling. No matter what happened in the future, she could not regret her engagement, not when it had made Ed happy.

Chapter Five

Dwight stared at the door to the operating theater, frowning when it did not open. Where was she? Breakfast had been over for hours, or so it seemed. She should be here. Just because the other staff hadn't arrived didn't mean there were no men to treat. Didn't Carolyn realize that they had important work to do? Men's lives were at stake, and she was late. Dwight thrust his hands into his pockets when he realized he had balled them in frustration. He couldn't let Carolyn—or anyone—annoy him that much.

If it were another nurse, Dwight would have thought she was fussing with her hair, but—though she was the prettiest woman Dwight had ever seen—Carolyn appeared to spend no time primping. He had never seen her look in a mirror or try to catch her reflection in a window the way Louise and his sisters did. Dwight was certain curling her hair wasn't the reason Carolyn was late. Knowing her, she was joking with someone in the wards. That wasn't necessarily bad. Even though Dwight put no credence in the therapeutic effects of laughter, the men in the wards appreciated Carolyn and her jokes. The problem was, men *needed* her here. He needed her, for until she arrived, he could do nothing.

He couldn't ask the orderlies to bring in his first patient, because without a nurse, he was unable to operate.

Dwight frowned again. Where was she? He had been waiting for what felt like hours, and she was—he blinked when he saw the clock. It must have stopped. He reached for his watch, shaking his head when it registered the same time as the stately grandfather clock. There was no denying the evidence. Carolyn wasn't late. He was early.

How odd. Today, he had felt an unusual sense of anticipation when he had wakened. That must have been the reason he'd rushed through breakfast without being aware of how quickly he must have eaten. It was surely the thought of saving more lives that had brought him here ahead of schedule. It couldn't be anything else. It most definitely could not have been a desire to see Clothespin Carolyn's smile.

As the other doctors began to arrive, the energy level in the operating theater increased, and the orderlies wheeled in the first patients. Still, there was no sign of Carolyn. And then the door opened, and she whirled inside. That was the only way to describe her entrance, for she was practically running, and that lovely golden hair bounced against her cheeks, while she bestowed a warm smile on each man that she passed. She was beautiful and so filled with vitality that it was difficult not to smile in return. Dwight didn't smile, of course. That would not be seemly, particularly not here in the operating room. He wouldn't want the injured men to think he regarded them with anything less than complete seriousness. As Carolyn smiled again, Dwight bit the inside of his mouth to keep his lips from turning up.

Two of the men who lay on stretchers waiting for their turn in surgery did more than smile. They whistled their appreciation.

"Gentlemen." Carolyn gave them an obviously false frown. That pretty heart-shaped face radiated joy, despite the down-turned lips. "My granny would say that you had indulged in inappropriate behavior. A gentleman never whistles inside a building."

The man with the head wound grinned. "Can't a fella say you're the prettiest sight he's seen since he left home? You're worth gettin' wounded for."

Carolyn shook her head. Though her hair bounced, the starched cap remained firmly perched on top of her head. "My granny always told me flattery was like cod liver oil. A little is good for you, but you don't want to overdo."

While Dwight struggled to maintain his solemnity, the soldier laughed. "My granny never told me nurses were like you."

They're not, Dwight wanted to say. Instead, he said only, "Nurse, please prepare this man for surgery." He nodded at the first man who had whistled. Judging from his badly lacerated arm, fragments of a shell had hit Corporal Miller. The man's chart indicated that he was from the American Expeditionary Force. "I see you're part of the Big Red One," Dwight said, using the nickname the soldiers had given to the US First Division.

"Yes, sir!" Corporal Miller started to salute, then winced when his arm refused to move. "You gonna take off my arm?"

"Not if I can help it."

Though Dwight thought he had sounded confident, Miller's expression was dubious. Carolyn laid a hand on his uninjured arm. "You can trust Dr. Hollins," she said, her voice low and soothing.

"But what if he can't save it?"

"He will!" Dwight wished he were as confident as Carolyn. He had amputated far too many limbs since this war had begun. All he could do was pray that the statesmen were right and that this was truly the war to end all wars. If this was the last time men had to fight, perhaps all the suffering Dwight had seen would not be in vain.

Carolyn reached for the chloroform. "You can trust the

doctor." As she prepared to slide the mask over Corporal Miller's face, she gave him a conspiratorial smile. "My granny always said you could tell a mule's character by the shape of his ears and a man's by the shape of his thumbs." She nodded toward Dwight. "Dr. Hollins has honest thumbs."

It was all Dwight could do not to laugh. He had never heard anything so absurd in his entire life. But the patient was less critical. He let out a full-bodied laugh. "That's good," Carolyn said with another of those smiles that must have charmed the young men in Texas. "Laughter can heal almost as well as medicine."

"If you say so, Nurse." Corporal Miller closed his eyes and relaxed. Dwight shook his head slightly. Though Carolyn's techniques were distinctly unconventional, he had to admit they worked.

"Did your grandmother live with you?" he asked when they had sutured the corporal's wounds. Although he normally spoke only to demand another instrument or bandage, Dwight was feeling almost ebullient at the fact that he had saved the man's arm. Miller would return home able to wrap both arms around his sweetheart. Sweetheart? Where had that thought come from? Dwight hadn't been thinking of Louise.

"What makes you think that?"

For a second, Dwight stared at Carolyn, wondering how she had known he was thinking about sweethearts. Then he realized she was responding to his question about her grandmother. "You quote her so often," Dwight said, hoping his relief that she was not a mind reader was not obvious. He didn't need anyone—especially Carolyn—knowing the direction his thoughts had taken. "I figured you must have spent a lot of time with your grandmother."

Carolyn blushed. Her lips parted as if she were going to speak, but before any words could emerge, she clamped them together.

Though Dwight raised one brow, trying to encourage her, she remained silent. By the time she had anesthetized a man with a head wound but had uttered not one word, Dwight was annoyed. Was she playing a game, reminding him that he was normally taciturn? Pettiness like that seemed out of character for Carolyn.

When her lips quivered again, Dwight could stand it no longer. "It's obvious you want to say something. Do it."

She shook her head and handed him the forceps he'd requested. "You told me to think before speaking or acting. I simply took your advice."

He grimaced. "Is this a case of 'be careful what you ask for'?" When Carolyn shrugged, Dwight suspected she had no intention of responding to his original question. "At this point, whatever you say can hardly be classified as impulsive," he told her. Though he'd been mildly curious about her grandmother when he'd posed his question, now Dwight felt an almost irrational need to know how the older woman had influenced Carolyn. "You've had plenty of time to think and to phrase your answer as carefully as an attorney." Dwight looked down at his patient, annoyed when he realized how distracted he was. "Come on, Carolyn. What's the problem? All I did was ask was a simple question."

"But the answer's not so simple." Another blush stained her cheeks. Dwight wondered if she realized how becoming that blush was. Even when frowning, Carolyn was a beautiful woman, but with the faint color on her face and those sparkling blue eyes . . . Dwight clenched his jaw, attempting to repress thoughts that were decidedly inappropriate.

"Promise you won't tell anyone?" she asked. She looked around the room, as if trying to assure herself that no one would overhear her. But the rest of the staff, unlike Dwight, was too busy treating the wounded to care about Carolyn's revelation.

Dwight nodded his assent. "And if you're wondering

whether you can trust me, remember that you're the one who said I have honest thumbs." He couldn't help the smile that crossed his face at the memory of her absurd declaration. It was just another dreary day in Goudot, with rain pelting the windows. The coal shortage had worsened, and now even the operating theater, which had been reasonably warm yesterday, felt frigid. Yet the dismal conditions had seemed to fade when Carolyn told her tales. Honest thumbs! What an idea!

"That's the problem."

Dwight quirked an eyebrow. "You mean you were wrong, and I don't have honest thumbs?"

"No." As she glanced at his hands, another blush rose to her cheeks. "That is . . ." Carolyn swallowed deeply, then blurted out the words, "I don't know . . ."

"You mean your grandmother really didn't teach you how to judge thumbs and mules' ears?"

Carolyn shook her head. "My grandmother didn't teach me anything. Both of my grandmothers died before I was born."

Her response surprised him, as she must have known it would. Once again, Clothespin Carolyn had done the unpredictable. "Then all those granny stories . . ."

"Were just that: stories."

"Let me guess. You invented the grandmother and her homilies on an impulse." That seemed to be the way Carolyn got through life, doing whatever seemed best at the time.

"Exactly." Judging from the expression on her face, she had no regrets, other than the fact that he'd revealed her deception. "I wanted to make the soldiers laugh." Her eyes were somber as she continued. "Haven't you noticed that no one thinks young women are funny? If I had told the same stories and admitted they were mine, no one would have been amused. So I invented a wise old grandmother."

It wasn't, Dwight had to admit, a bad idea. "Let me look

at your hands." Obviously puzzled by the request, she held them out for his inspection. They were small, almost delicate, with graceful fingers. And one of those fingers bore an engagement ring. Dwight started to frown, then stopped himself. Of course, she was engaged. He'd known that from the first day she'd assisted him.

"Is something wrong?" she asked.

He nodded solemnly. "I was right." He paused for effect, then added, "*You* don't have honest thumbs."

Carolyn's eyes widened in obvious surprise. "You made a joke, Doctor Hollins." There was a note of wonderment in her voice.

"Why, so I did." Dwight looked down at the man on the stretcher. It hadn't hurt either him or his patient. Maybe Carolyn was right. Maybe humor had its place.

In her dream, someone was ill, violently ill. Carolyn turned and pulled the pillow over her head, willing the dream to go away. But the sounds continued, retching punctuated with soft moans of pain. It was no dream! Carolyn's eyes flew open and she sat up, tossing the pillow aside as she realized that Helen was in agony.

"What's wrong?" she asked, lighting a lamp. The only thing worse than being sick was being sick in the dark. She wondered how long her roommate had been huddled over a basin. In Carolyn's dream, the sounds had gone on forever, but dream time, Carolyn knew, often bore no relation to real time. Perhaps it had been only a few seconds.

"Do you think the fish was spoiled?" Carolyn had never acquired a taste for fish and had refused last night's main course.

Helen shook her head, then wiped her face and turned to Carolyn. "I'm not sick," she said with a weak smile. Though she was pale, her brown eyes sparkled with what looked like happiness. "Promise you won't tell anyone."

Carolyn nodded, remembering how, less than a day

earlier, she had extracted the same promise from Dwight. Whatever secret Helen wanted her to keep, she suspected it was more important than an imaginary grandmother.

Helen reached for the pitcher they filled each evening and poured herself a glass of water. When she'd taken a sip, the smile she gave Carolyn was radiant. "I'm pregnant," she announced.

Pregnant! No wonder Helen had been sick so many mornings. Carolyn had attributed that and Helen's complaints of fatigue to the schedule they both kept. But Helen's malady wasn't a malady at all. Instead, it was a reason for celebration. In the midst of this horrible war, a new life had begun.

"That's wonderful!" Carolyn hugged her friend, then studied her with new eyes. Helen was to be a mother. How exciting! "You must be thrilled."

"I am." Helen smiled again as she cranked the shutters open. The pale light of another rainy dawn brightened the room only slightly. "The one thing I'm sorry about is that I won't be able to stay here much longer. Miss Pierce will send me home as soon as she knows."

Carolyn didn't doubt it. The head nurse was not one to bend rules without a direct order. "She'll find out eventually."

"I know that." Helen looked down at her still slim figure, and Carolyn suspected she was imagining the inevitable changes. "All I want to do is postpone it as long as possible. Somehow, I need to hide the morning sickness from her."

Carolyn nodded and suggested that she could take Helen's early morning shift. "I'll do whatever I can for you." Carolyn hugged her friend again. "This is so exciting!" Though nothing short of a truce would end the horrible injuries and death they dealt with every day, it was wonderful to know that the circle of life continued.

"It feels like a miracle," Helen admitted. She sank onto

the room's one chair, as if the effort of opening the shutters had tired her.

"What does Glen think?" Carolyn asked, referring to Helen's husband. She knew they'd been married for three years and that one of the reasons Helen had volunteered to come to France was that her husband was stationed on the Western Front. The baby must have been the result of a brief leave that they'd managed to share the week before Carolyn had come to the hospital.

Helen had told Carolyn that they had rendezvoused in Paris and that the French capital was as beautiful as she had dreamed, even though the mood was even grimmer there than in Goudot, as the Parisians feared an enemy occupation. The journey, too, had been fraught with difficulties. Though Paris was only one hundred kilometers from Goudot as the crow flies, Helen had explained that there were neither crow flights available nor any direct routes, and so the sixty-six miles had become close to one hundred. "But it was worth it!" she had declared. Now that visit must seem even more wonderful.

"Is Glen as excited as you?"

To Carolyn's surprise, a shadow crossed Helen's face. "I haven't told him." As Carolyn raised an eyebrow, Helen continued, "We had two false starts, so I want to be sure before I tell him." She smiled at Carolyn. "You're the only one who knows."

A lump formed in Carolyn's throat at the thought that this woman who'd been a stranger a month before now trusted her with such an important secret. "Thank you, Helen. I promise I won't betray your confidence."

Helen reached forward and laid a hand on Carolyn's arm. "I know you won't. You're the most loyal person I've ever met."

Though she couldn't have explained why, Helen's words transported Carolyn back to Canela, and she pictured Ed's face the day she'd agreed to marry him. He had been happier than she'd ever seen him. And she? Carolyn couldn't remember how she had felt other than the pleasure of knowing that she could help Ed. It was not unlike what she felt today, knowing she could help Helen. How odd. Was *loyalty* what she felt for Ed?

"You're late, Carolyn." Dwight stood next to the operating table, his hazel eyes cold with anger. "You're late," he repeated.

She knew she was, but she couldn't regret it, not under the circumstances. If she had her way, this particular operation would be delayed even more. Today, for the first time since she had come to Goudot, so many injured men had been brought to the hospital that they had overflowed the wards and were lined up in the hallways. Carolyn glanced at the three men who were waiting for surgery and flashed them her most brilliant smile, hoping they'd understand what she was about to do. Though their faces were lined with pain and worry, the patients managed to return her smile. Dwight, however, did not smile. The steely look he gave her was as disapproving as his words.

"Sorry, Doctor," she said as she approached him. Keeping her tone light, she said, "I know I'm late, but I had to dance with one of my beaux." If only that were true!

The patients chuckled. The doctor did not. "That is not amusing. Now, if you can take time away from your dancing schedule to assist me . . ." He gestured toward the instrument tray.

She had to make him understand, and she had to do it quickly. "Actually, Doctor Hollins, I thought perhaps I could convince you to waltz with me."

His frown deepened. "Have you taken leave of your senses?" he demanded.

"I don't believe so." She twirled as if she were ending a dance, then looked pointedly at the door. He had to understand.

"May I have a word with you?" His annoyance was growing.

"Yes, sir. Perhaps in the hallway." Without giving him a chance to respond, she left the operating theater. A second later Dwight was next to her, his face suffused with anger.

"Will you kindly explain what that charade was all about?" Though his fury was palpable, Dwight kept his voice low so that the waiting men would not overhear him.

There was no time for explanations. Carolyn grabbed Dwight's hand and began to hurry along the corridor, nodding at the men whose stretchers lined one side. They had been arranged in order of the severity of their wounds. Though Dwight tried to protest, she would not loosen her grip. "There's a man who can't wait," she said as softly as she could.

"Are you questioning our triage?" he demanded.

"No, Doctor, I'm not. I think this man's injury was not apparent when he was brought in." They had reached the tenth stretcher. Though the other patients were all conscious, this man was not. He was unnaturally pale, and his skin was cold and clammy.

Dwight reached for the man's hand, checking his pulse. "He's in shock." The words confirmed Carolyn's fears. Two orderlies were tending to patients at the end of the corridor. "Get this man into the theater now!" Dwight shouted. As he and Carolyn hurried back into the operating room, the frown had disappeared. "That was good thinking, Carolyn," he said, his voice once more warm with approval. "What I don't understand is why you didn't just tell me what was wrong."

That was simple. Carolyn had seen what fear did to people, how it could lower defenses that were already dangerously low because of wounds. "It would have upset the men who were waiting for you. They'll know there's a problem when they see the new patient brought in, but at least you'll be there to reassure them." If she and Dwight had left without an explanation—even one as silly as his need to reprimand her for her frivolity—the men would have imagined disasters far worse than the truth.

Twelve hours later, Carolyn and Dwight entered the ward to check on the patients who had been in surgery that morning. Though it had been an arduous day, they had been lucky and had lost no patients. Dwight had discovered that the man who had been in shock had internal bleeding, and he had been able to stop it in time. Equally encouraging, though they had been forced to perform several of the amputations they both hated, they had all been successful.

"Is the doc a good dancer?" The question came from one of the men who had been awaiting surgery when Carolyn had invited Dwight to waltz. Apparently he remembered the ploy Carolyn had used to get Dwight out of the room.

"No!" Dwight's response was immediate.

Carolyn winked at the patient. "The doctor thinks dancing is frivolous. You and I know better."

The man winked back. "I'll bet he's looking forward to dancing at your wedding."

Her wedding. Carolyn still couldn't form a mental picture of that day. "I wasn't planning to invite him."

"And I wasn't planning to attend," Dwight added.

To her surprise, the patients laughed.

"Did you hear that, Jake?" one demanded.

"Sure did, but I don't believe it."

The man named Jake grinned at Carolyn. "You two act just like the missus and me, and you're not even married."

"What do you mean?" Dwight demanded at the same time that Carolyn said, "You thought we . . ."

"That's preposterous." Dwight words blended with Carolyn's as she said, "Of course not!"

Jake shook his head. "You can't fool us, not with that sparkler on your hand." He pointed at Carolyn's ring. "The missus always said I don't notice much, but I reckon I know an engagement ring when I see it."

Suddenly, Carolyn understood why the men were laughing. And, though perhaps it shouldn't have mattered, it somehow seemed vital that they know the truth. She, the woman who had invented a wise old grandmother, wanted no misunderstandings on this subject. "You're right," she agreed. "I am engaged."

"As am I," Dwight admitted.

Jake turned toward the other men. "I told you so!" There was no disguising the triumph in his voice.

He thought he understood, but he was mistaken—badly mistaken. When Jake was once more looking at her, Carolyn shook her head slowly. "The doctor and I are engaged," she said, "but not to each other."

He winked. "Oh, I get it. No one's supposed to know."

"Must be some Army regulation," another chimed in.

"Your secret's safe with us," Jake declared. He turned and addressed his fellow patients. "Right, boys?"

"Right."

Though the men all nodded solemnly, when someone began to hum 'The Wedding March,' the rest joined in.

"Send us a piece of cake," one cried.

"I wanna dance with the bride," another announced.

"Dance? I wanna kiss the bride."

Her cheeks flaming, Carolyn did not dare to look at Dwight. It was, as he had said, preposterous. And yet, try though she might to deny it, the image of herself and Dwight standing in front of a church, exchanging vows and rings, danced before her eyes.

Preposterous!

Chapter Six

Surgery was easy compared to this. Dwight shook his head as he entered the last of the shops on Goudot's main street. The letters painted on the plate glass window said *Épicerie*. Dwight wasn't certain what that meant, but judging from the enticing aromas that wafted through the air, it had something to do with food. Though food wasn't what he had had in mind, desperation was a strong motivator.

What had made him think he could do this? He was a physician, a man trained to heal others. As a farmer's son, he had learned to do many things, from milking a cow to repairing a plow. Dwight could do those, and—if he said so himself—could do them passably well. Unfortunately, setting broken bones and herding cows into the barn did not prepare him for today's tasks. It was bad enough that his French accent made the shopkeepers smile. He could handle that. The problem was, he had no idea what to do once he entered the shops. In all his twenty-seven years, he had never had to do this alone.

The épicerie was no different from the other establishments he had entered. Dwight stared at the counters of merchandise, as bewildered as if he were on a distant planet, confronted with the artifacts of a strange society. *"Non, merci,"* he said as he retreated. This was not a good idea. Though his family would be disappointed if he failed in this mission, he saw no way of bringing it to a successful conclusion. He had once told Carolyn that he planned his life as completely as General Pershing planned his military campaigns. Wouldn't she laugh if she could see him today? He was definitely not winning this campaign.

It had seemed like such a good idea when he had left the hospital. He would actually take an afternoon off—the first since he had arrived—and would visit the town. Dwight knew from the other doctors' comments that Goudot was small, but he had also heard that the stores were surprisingly well stocked for a town of five hundred, particularly for wartime. Surely one of those stores would have what he needed.

The town was a little over a mile from the hospital. Dwight shook his head as he reminded himself that the French measured distance in kilometers. The town was two kilometers from the hospital. Though the road was cratered, the result of some aerial bombing that had occurred last year, Dwight had enjoyed the walk along the tree-lined route. French roads, he had discovered, were frequently lined with tall, slender trees. Poplars, he had heard someone call them. The enjoyment he had found in the walk had ended when he had entered the first shop.

Dwight turned up the collar of his coat against the wind and headed back toward the hospital. There at least he knew what was expected of him. Unlike the dismal failure today's expedition had proven to be, he was successful at the hospital.

Dwight had taken two steps when he saw her. Though she wore the same dark woollen uniform as the other nurses, there was no mistaking that golden hair or the graceful way she walked. Unlike him, Carolyn appeared to have no problem shopping, for she had emerged from the butcher shop with a tightly wrapped package.

"Carolyn!" He didn't bother to disguise the pleasure in his voice as he crossed the street to join her. At least now he'd have something to think about other than his failures. Dwight sniffed Carolyn's package appreciatively. "What is that? It smells delicious." It was ridiculous to feel happy, simply because he was standing on a cobblestone street talking to the prettiest nurse in all of France, but Dwight could not deny the elation that surged through him.

"I bought some sausage." Carolyn peeled back the paper and let the aroma waft onto the air. "I told the cook I'd help her make stuffing for Thanksgiving, even if we are going to stuff goose instead of turkeys."

Dwight grimaced, remembering the cries of anguish he'd heard two of the other doctors emit when they learned that there were no turkeys to be found for the traditional feast. Dwight hadn't understood the fuss then, and he didn't now. They were in the midst of a war, for goodness sake. What was important was stopping the killing and getting the men home. Besides, he wasn't sure there were many reasons to give thanks this year. Though the French and English had hoped that America's entry into the war would ensure an Allied victory, it had been more than six months since President Wilson had declared war, and the tide had yet to turn.

Carolyn must have misunderstood his frown, for twin furrows appeared between her eyes. "Don't you like sausage in your stuffing?"

Dwight shook his head, then nodded, not sure which question he was answering. "I like stuffing and gravy," he admitted. He looked down the street, a little surprised that he and Carolyn were the only people outside. When he had arrived, he had seen a few elderly men and a number of women dressed in the unrelieved black that appeared to be their favorite color.

Carolyn unwrapped the sausage. "The patients are more excited about the meal preparations than I would have thought possible. It's all they can talk about when I go into the wards." She smiled as if the memory of the men's excitement was a pleasant one. "That's one of the reasons I asked my sister to send our mother's recipe for sausage stuffing. It's the best."

Chastened by her explanation, Dwight managed a smile of his own. "Then we'll have one reason to be thankful."

"We have many," Carolyn countered. "For one thing, the rain has stopped."

As a black-clad woman approached the butcher shop, Dwight stepped out of the way. "It may not be raining, but now it's snowing." Although only a dusting had fallen overnight, lazy flakes were continuing to drift downward, and the road was turning white. He hadn't minded the snow when he had been on the dirt road, but the cobblestones that paved the center of town would soon be slippery.

"Ed says the men are hoping the ground will freeze. Those who were here last winter claim that's better than living with mud."

Ed. Dwight tried not to react to the man's name. Of course Carolyn would speak of her fiancé. Of course her view of the war would be centered on him. That was only natural. Dwight understood that. It must be something he'd eaten that made a lump form in his stomach. It couldn't be anything else.

Trying to regain his composure, he studied the buildings that formed the center of Goudot. They couldn't have been more different from the stores at home. Those were simple wood-framed buildings. These were three stories high, constructed of stone and far from simple, for each had gracefully curved windows set into the roofs. The buildings at home were white-washed. Like the sky on a rainy day, these were gray, with darker gray slate roofs. What surprised Dwight the most was that, while the stores at home sprawled on large lots, these were narrow and were all attached, like the Philadelphia row houses he'd seen in a drawing. Goudot bore virtually no resemblance to an Iowa farm town.

Though Dwight had no intention of discussing Ed, he wanted to continue his conversation with Carolyn. "The snow is actually the reason I'm here," he told her. "It reminded me that Christmas is next month and I'd better buy my gifts."

She looked pointedly at his empty hands. "It doesn't appear that you've been buying anything."

"That's the heart of the matter." Dwight blinked. Why was he speaking of hearts? He should have said *crux,* not *heart.* Hoping Carolyn didn't notice anything odd about his choice of words, he continued, "I can't decide what to get." He considered her smile encouragement. "I don't suppose you'd take pity on me, would you? Buying gifts for nine women is a daunting proposition." The second the words were out of his mouth, Dwight regretted them. Why was he speaking of propositions? He should have said *prospect.* Like *crux,* it had less emotional baggage attached to it.

Carolyn did not seem to notice his discomfort. "My shopping seems easy compared to that."

"You sound as if you're done."

As she brushed a snowflake off the tip of her nose, Dwight remembered how she'd looked wearing a clothespin. Her nose looked much better unadorned. "I am finished shopping. Are you surprised?"

"Will you refuse to help me if I admit that I am?" He had thought that Carolyn, a woman who clearly did not believe in advance planning, would buy her gifts at the last minute.

She shook her head. "And deprive myself of some fun? Not likely."

"Fun? You call shopping fun?"

With a little shrug, she said, "It's one thing I'm good at." She wasn't boasting. In fact, it sounded almost as if she were apologizing. How odd. She was good at so many things; and yet she seemed unaware of that.

Dwight wondered why. He wouldn't ask, though, and risk alienating her. Instead he said, "You've given me another reason to be thankful. Now I won't have to disappoint my family. That's who I'm shopping for."

"How old are your sisters?" When Dwight told her their ages, Carolyn tipped her head to one side, apparently trying to decide on appropriate gifts. "Hats and gloves," she announced a few seconds later. "There's not a girl alive who wouldn't love a new French hat."

Dwight looked at Carolyn's head, suddenly aware that she was wearing a hat. She was right, he realized. Women did wear hats, and his sisters wouldn't have to have theirs chosen by the Army or the Red Cross the way Carolyn did.

She led Dwight to a small store where—judging from the proprietor's warm greeting—she was well known. *"Bonjour, Madame,"* Carolyn said. Dwight looked around, wondering how he had missed this shop. Though the display window was small, it held three pieces of cloth and ribbon that appeared to be hats. For a moment, the two women chattered in French, with Carolyn gesturing toward the display of hats.

"Certainement, mademoiselle," the shopkeeper said. With an assessing look at Dwight, she pulled a deep purple turban from its stand, then pointed at Carolyn's hat, obviously telling her to remove it so that she could try on the new one.

For the next half hour, Carolyn tried on one hat after another, modeling each for Dwight, telling him which one she thought each of his sisters would like, given her age and the snippets of information he'd provided about his siblings. For a man who detested the very thought of shopping, spending so much time in an establishment that catered to women should have been a painful experience. It was not. In fact, Dwight could not remember when he had laughed more, for Carolyn's light-hearted approach to life obviously extended to shopping. As she tried on each of the hats, she would tilt her head from side to side, letting him see the headpiece from all angles. They had laughed when one of the turbans—which Madame insisted were the latest style—slipped down Carolyn's forehead and covered her eyes, and they had both found the stuffed bird perched on top of a straw hat highly amusing.

"I never knew shopping could be so much fun," Dwight admitted as they left the store, his arms now filled with parcels. And he had never known that hats could be so attractive.

"That's because you never went shopping with me," Carolyn said, her blue eyes sparkling with mirth. She brushed another snowflake from her nose. "You said you needed nine gifts. I assume one of the others is for your mother."

Dwight nodded. "Any suggestions?"

It was Carolyn's turn to nod. "Jewelry. Madame Fouquet has some lovely pieces." She led the way back to one of the stores he had entered earlier that afternoon. At the time, he had seen nothing that appealed to him. As had happened in the hat shop, Carolyn spent a minute explaining their mission, and the woman who had regarded him with skepticism only an hour before began to smile.

"Of course," she said and pulled out a tray of pendants.

"I thought your mother might like a lavaliere," Carolyn said, pointing to a long chain with what appeared to be gold tassels hanging from a disc that had many holes punched in it. "The filigreed one is particularly beautiful." Dwight looked at the piece of jewelry. Was that what the holes were called—filigree?

Carolyn fastened the chain around her neck so that Dwight could admire it. "Very nice." If the necklace—he couldn't pronounce the French word that Carolyn had used—looked half as pretty on his mother as it did on Carolyn, it would be a success. "Now all that's left is a gift for Louise. What would you suggest?"

Carolyn blinked. "Shouldn't you choose that yourself?"

Didn't she understand? It wasn't a matter of *should*. The simple fact was, he couldn't pick Louise's gift. "I have no idea what she wants."

"What did you give her last year?" Carolyn asked.

"Her engagement ring. But she selected that. She and I always bought her gifts together."

For a second Carolyn stared at him, speechless. There was something in her expression that made him think she pitied him. That was absurd, of course. There was no reason anyone would pity him. He was a well-respected physician, engaged to marry a perfectly suitable young woman.

"I see," Carolyn said at last. "I suppose Louise doesn't like surprises."

"Of course not. She'd rather get something she likes." Dwight had to admit he'd been relieved when Louise had suggested they shop together. Until then, one of his sisters had always gone with him to choose gifts for their mother and the other girls. That wasn't quite the same as selecting your own presents, but Dwight had been so thankful that he wouldn't have to endure the ordeal alone that he hadn't questioned Louise's suggestion.

Carolyn gave him another long look. "I see," she said again. Then she smiled brightly. "Is her hair long or short?"

It wasn't a difficult question. Dwight knew that. The problem was, he couldn't remember. For some reason, when he closed his eyes, he could not conjure his fiancée's image. All he could see was Carolyn's face, those blue eyes that sparkled more than the summer sky and the golden blonde hair that framed a perfectly beautiful face. Carolyn's hair was short. Dwight knew that. He could also describe the way it waved. That must be the latest style. Louise probably had short hair, too.

"Short," he said, hoping he sounded more confident than he felt.

"Then perhaps she would like ear bobs." As the proprietor showed them another tray of jewelry, Carolyn picked a set of earrings and held them next to her face. "If Louise doesn't like these, you can give them to your mother," she explained. "They match the lavaliere."

Dwight wasn't certain Louise would like ear bobs, or whatever it was Carolyn had called them. "Do you have any other suggestions?" He couldn't admit that he was having difficulty picturing any of the pieces of jewelry on Louise. Admitting that would mean admitting that he couldn't remember exactly what she looked like, and that was an admission he did not want to make. A man ought to be able to describe the woman he intended to marry.

Carolyn walked around the store, looking at the items on display. "These enamel brooches are pretty." She pointed to one that was embossed with flowers. Although it was delicate, the colors were vivid. Dwight was certain Louise would not wear it, for she had told him that colored stones were vulgar when he had mentioned that he liked sapphires.

"Not that one," he said, and this time there was no hesitation in his voice.

"Then take the ear bobs."

When the proprietor had wrapped the gifts, Dwight turned to Carolyn. "Can I buy you a cup of coffee as a thank you?" It was common courtesy, the least he could offer her after she had made his shopping excursion so pleasant. And if being courteous meant that the afternoon didn't have to end yet, well . . . that wasn't bad.

Carolyn nodded, her smile warming him more than a crackling fire. "I'd enjoy that."

That night when he was back in his room, Dwight could remember nothing that they had said as they had sat at a small table in the town's one pastry shop. They had talked for an hour, chatting about everything and nothing at the same time. It should have been boring. It should have felt like a waste of time. But it did not. Though he could recall none of the conversation, he had enjoyed every second of the time he had spent with Carolyn. For a few minutes, he had forgotten there was a war, and if that wasn't magic, he didn't know what was.

"You look happy," Helen said as Carolyn entered their room. "Did you get a letter from Ed?"

Carolyn shook her head, then draped her cape over a hook. It was still too wet to be hung in the armoire. "I went shopping."

A chuckle greeted her announcement. "No wonder you're smiling. That's every woman's favorite way to spend an afternoon off."

"It's even more fun when you're spending someone else's money. I felt like Santa, or maybe I should say like Mrs. Claus, buying Christmas presents."

"Dare I ask whose money you were spending?" Helen leaned back in the rocking chair that she had found in an attic and dragged to their room.

"Dwight's."

The rocking stopped abruptly. "Dwight . . . as in, Hollins?" There was no disguising Helen's surprise. Carolyn could feel her cheeks begin to flush. You'd think she had done something criminal rather than simply spending an enjoyable afternoon.

"The man has seven sisters," she said as evenly as she could. "He needed some help choosing gifts."

Helen narrowed her eyes, as if considering Carolyn's words. "I didn't think Hollow Heart would admit he needed anything."

A month ago, Carolyn would have laughed at the sobriquet. Today it annoyed her. "He's not that bad," she told her roommate. The truth was, she could not recall when she had spent a more pleasant three hours. Certainly not

since she had come to France. Even thinking back to her
life in Canela, though she could remember being happy,
she could not recall a conversation as enjoyable as the one
she'd shared with Dwight. He was not a hollow-hearted
man.

For a long moment, Helen said nothing but continued to
stare at Carolyn. "I see," she said at last, and the look she
gave Carolyn made her want to lower her gaze. There was
nothing to be embarrassed about. She had spent a few
pleasant hours with Dwight. That was all.

From the first time she had met him, Carolyn had admired his skill in the operating room; today simply proved
that he had a life outside of medicine, that—contrary to the
nurses' belief—he was not emotionless. There was absolutely no reason for Carolyn to feel so defensive about the
fact that she had spent her time off with Dwight. No reason
at all.

The next morning Carolyn entered the dining room an
hour earlier than usual. Though she had skipped breakfast
several of the mornings when she had taken Helen's first
shift, she was hungry today. For some reason she had spent
a restless night, plagued by dreams of weddings and
grooms whose faces were suddenly transformed when she
approached the front of the church. It was absurd, of
course, that none of them had looked like Ed. He was going
to be her groom.

When she had filled her plate, Carolyn looked for an
empty chair. The dining room was surprisingly crowded.
The long table that the nurses normally shared was full,
although there was a table near them with an open spot.
Carolyn headed in that direction. As she did, she passed by
a table for two occupied by only one man. It would be rude
not to greet him.

"Good morning, Doctor Hollins." Though she had had
no intention of sitting at his table, he rose and pulled out

the chair opposite him. It would be inexcusably rude to refuse. She did not.

"My name is Dwight," he said softly when she was seated.

"I know." In her thoughts he was always "Dwight," so much so that she had to make a conscious effort to remember to address him formally. Yesterday, because she had not wanted to remind either of them of the hospital, she had been careful not to use any name at all, even though he called her Carolyn.

"Then why don't you use my name? And before you tell me it wouldn't be seemly, I agree that we're Doctor and Nurse when we're in the operating room."

"All right . . . Dwight."

"That didn't hurt, did it?"

Carolyn laughed. "Not much." But she wasn't laughing a minute later when he asked her to pass the salt. Their fingertips touched as she handed him the salt dish, and the spark that traveled up her arm was stronger than the shock she had once received when she'd touched a wire with wet hands. The electric shock had been painful; this was not. Instead, though it surprised her by its intensity, she found it oddly pleasant, an experience she would like to repeat.

Her sister Martha had told both Carolyn and Emily that they would know when they had met the man they were destined to marry, for they'd feel a pull as strong as the most powerful magnet, and the man's slightest touch would make sparks fly. Both Carolyn and Emily had believed Martha was exaggerating. Now Carolyn wasn't so certain. This was unlike anything she had ever experienced. What she didn't understand was why it was Dwight who was generating sparks. It should be Ed. After all, Ed was the man she was going to marry.

The rest of the meal was uneventful, for Carolyn was careful to touch only the edges of the dishes she passed to Dwight, and by the time they entered the operating room, she had convinced herself that she had imagined the sparks. It *had* been her imagination, she realized when they reached the end of the shift and the odd electrical current had not recurred, though she had handed Dwight dozens of instruments and bandages, and their hands had touched more than once. Thank goodness!

Perhaps it was also her imagination that they worked together more smoothly than ever before. From the beginning, Carolyn had found it easy to work with Dwight. Helen, who had seen them operating, had told Carolyn that they looked like dancers in a perfectly choreographed ballet. Today, however, even the slightest hesitation was gone. Carolyn knew exactly what Dwight was going to need, and she handed it to him before he could telegraph his request. Though he said nothing, she sensed that he was pleased with their performance.

When the last patient had been treated, Dwight stripped off his mask and turned to Carolyn. "Thank you, Nurse," he said, obviously remembering his promise of formality in the operating theater. "I've never seen such flawless work."

One of the blushes that seemed to come so often stained Carolyn's cheeks. "You make it easy," she told Dwight, trying to return some of the pleasure his compliment had given her. "You always do things in exactly the same way."

The corners of his mouth turned up. "Then you admit that planning has its merits?"

Carolyn removed and folded her apron, thankful that she was not the one who had to launder it. "I never said it didn't."

"But you still prefer spontaneity."

She nodded. "It has its place," she agreed, "but I'd be the first to admit that an operating room is not that place."

The smile that had been teasing Dwight's lips turned into a full-fledged grin. "We've agreed twice in as many minutes. That calls for a celebration."

"What did you have in mind?" He still had rounds to do, and she had planned to visit the men in the wards.

"A cup of hot chocolate and some biscuits."

Carolyn wasn't certain which sounded more appealing, the food or the opportunity to sit down for a few minutes. "Biscuits? You sound English." Dwight shrugged and opened the door for her. As they entered the long hallway that led past the wards, he said, "I can't pronounce the French word for pastry the way you can." He sounded as if he regretted his lack of fluency in French. That was silly. One man couldn't know everything.

"While you were learning to be a doctor and save lives," she told him, "I was taught to set a table, arrange flowers, and pronounce a few French phrases. Somehow I suspect your education has proven more valuable."

"Unless you live in Goudot and want one of those fancy lemon pies that we ate yesterday."

"The *tartes à citron?*" They had been delicious. As Carolyn spied a familiar uniform, she smiled. "I just saw something even better than lemon tarts: the mailman. Let's see what he's brought us." The mailman made two deliveries, the first to the wards, the second to the dining room. Although the staff normally picked up their mail in the dining room, if they happened to be in the wards, they would collect their letters there.

Ten minutes later, when Carolyn had slid envelopes from Theo and Ed into her pocket, she touched Dwight's arm. He was standing with his back to her, staring out the window as though fascinated by the sight of puddles. "Are you ready for hot chocolate?"

"May I give you a raincheck?"

Carolyn glanced outside, surprised at his suggestion. Anyone who had been in France for any length of time knew better than to delay activities until the rain stopped. "It's not raining very much." Besides, they were only walking to the other side of the courtyard. She looked back at

Dwight and saw that the gleam in his eyes had faded. "What's wrong?" she asked. When he did not answer, she took his arm and started walking toward the door. "You can tell me about it over chocolate. And don't say no or promise me a raincheck, because I won't accept either." A fine mist was falling as they crossed the courtyard. "My granny always said a man was no better than a sand burr if he didn't keep his word."

As she had hoped, her words brought a shadow of a smile to Dwight's face. "I'm afraid that I'm not acquainted with sand burrs."

"For which you can be thankful. Now, are you going to renege on your promise of chocolate?"

The smile broadened a bit, although it was still far short of a grin. "And risk being called a sand burr? No!"

When they had ordered their drinks and a plate of the pastries that the shop in Goudot delivered each afternoon, Carolyn leaned forward. "What was bothering you?" Though Dwight seemed happier, his eyes still reflected concern.

He shrugged, as if trying to minimize his worries. "This makes two weeks that I haven't gotten a letter from Louise, and that's not like her. She writes to me every Monday."

Carolyn kept a smile fixed on her face. She had heard about the schedule and had been surprised at the time. Carolyn doubted she would like a woman who didn't enjoy surprises and who planned every aspect of her life. But of course, it didn't matter whether she liked Louise. Carolyn would never meet her. It was Dwight who would spend the rest of his life with her. For her part, Carolyn couldn't imagine having such a regimented life, and she most certainly could not understand picking out her own Christmas gifts. Where was the fun in that? Christmas morning was a time for shaking and sniffing and guessing the contents of a package before it was unwrapped. But she said nothing more than, "There must be a delay in the mail from the

States." She wouldn't tell Dwight that her sisters' letters arrived regularly.

Furrows appeared between his eyes. "Unless something's wrong. Perhaps she's ill." He shook his head, dismissing that thought. "Her mother would tell me if she were ill."

There had to be another reason for the delay. "Did Louise say anything unusual in her last letter?"

Dwight was silent for a moment, appearing to consider her question. "Only that the Tin Lizzie needed another repair."

Carolyn couldn't help it. She laughed. "That's not unusual," she told him. "My sister Emily spends half her time fixing ours."

For the first time since they'd started the conversation, Dwight's face brightened. "Your sister works on automobiles?" he asked, clearly incredulous.

Carolyn smiled, remembering her younger sister's antics. "Emily always did whatever Theo did. You remember that they're twins, don't you?" When he nodded, she continued. "Emily wasn't very good at baseball because the boys wouldn't let her play on their team, but she's even better than Theo at figuring out how things work."

"You're an amazing family." Dwight's words were tinged with admiration.

"The others are," Carolyn corrected him. "Martha's smart. She can teach anyone anything. Theo's the most athletic person I've ever met, and I've told you Emily's a mechanical genius."

Dwight looked only moderately impressed by the list of her siblings' accomplishments. "What about you?"

"Me?" Carolyn thought that was obvious. "Everyone in Canela calls me the decorative one."

Dwight nodded. "I can't argue with their eyesight. You're the most beautiful woman I've ever seen." There was no flattery in his words, only what appeared to be a statement of facts. For some reason, Carolyn was more pleased by that than she had been by any of the fulsome compliments she had received from men at home.

"That's the problem," she told Dwight.

This time there was no doubt that she had surprised him. "I don't understand. I thought every woman wanted to be beautiful."

"I don't! Not if it means that everyone thinks that's all there is to me." When Dwight didn't seem startled by her outburst, she continued, "That's one of the reasons I volunteered for the war. I wanted to prove that I could be useful, not just a decoration to be brought out for parties." It was important that he understood.

To Carolyn's surprise, Dwight leaned across the table and took her hand in his. His hazel eyes darkened as he said, "Don't ever sell yourself short, Carolyn. You're smart and you're strong and you can do anything you set your mind to. I knew that the first time I saw you."

Carolyn stared at him, astonished. Not only had no one ever said that to her, but she had never thought of herself that way. Could it be true?

Chapter Seven

Carolyn wakened to the now familiar sound of Helen's morning sickness. The poor woman! This happened every day, without fail, and although Helen never complained, Carolyn could see the strain the nausea and the need to conceal it from the rest of the hospital staff were taking on her roommate.

Slipping her arms into her dressing gown, Carolyn padded toward her friend, who was sitting on her bed, wiping her face with a damp cloth. Carolyn lit a lamp, then poured a glass of water for Helen. "You and that son or daughter of yours sure know how to start the day." Carolyn kept her voice light, hoping either the water or her own cheerful attitude would help Helen feel better.

Her roommate swallowed carefully. "I've heard it will be over soon. I just hope that's true." For the first time, Helen's voice betrayed her discomfort. Though she had been so stoic about the continuous sickness that Carolyn had declared Helen was trying to prove that she possessed the stiffest of the proverbial English stiff upper lips, today that stiff upper lip was trembling.

"Think about it this way," Carolyn encouraged her. "You

can tell everyone the baby has Glen's black hair and your green face."

As she had hoped, Helen laughed. Bending over, she wrapped her arms around her stomach. "How can you do that to me?" she demanded, her voice still suffused with laughter. "Don't you know that it hurts to laugh?"

"Maybe so, but your cheeks are a more becoming color now." Though pale, they had lost the greenish hue that nausea gave them.

Helen took another sip of water, then fixed her gaze on Carolyn. "I wonder what the baby will look like." She touched her face self-consciously. "I hope he doesn't have my nose." Though Carolyn saw nothing wrong with Helen's nose, her friend complained about the fact that its tip turned up. She had even asked whether Carolyn thought a clothespin might cure the problem.

"Your baby will be beautiful," Carolyn said. Weren't all babies beautiful? That's what her sister Martha claimed.

"So will yours, when you have one."

Her baby. Carolyn closed her eyes for a second, trying to imagine herself as a mother. She could picture herself cradling an infant in her arms. It would be a little girl with brown hair, hazel eyes, and . . . Carolyn's eyes flew open as she realized that she had conjured the image of a miniature Dwight. How annoying! Her daughter would not look like Dwight. She would have Ed's red hair and green eyes. It was totally absurd to be imaging a child that looked like Dwight. Propinquity, Martha would call it. The effect of spending so much time in Dwight's company. It was that, nothing more.

"When are you going to tell Glen about the baby?" Carolyn asked, as much to take her mind off the thought of her own imaginary child as to help Helen focus on something other than her traitorous stomach.

A fond smile crossed Helen's face. "Christmas," she said. Carolyn knew that—like everyone else in the hospital—Helen hoped that there would be a holiday truce. If that happened, she and Glen would both be able to take leave and spend a few days together.

"Your news will be the only gift Glen remembers this year," she predicted.

"I hope so."

An hour later, Carolyn stood next to Dwight in the operating theater as the orderly carried in their first patient. The chart indicated that Corporal Frederick Seymour had a badly shattered femur and that amputation was recommended.

Carolyn uncovered the man's leg, then looked up at Dwight. Though she doubted Corporal Seymour noticed it, she knew Dwight's moods well enough to read concern in his expression.

"I'm gonna lose it, ain't I?" the man asked as Dwight examined the wound. Corporal Seymour's voice was filled with the resignation she heard so often, a mixture of relief that he was still alive and regret that life would never be the same.

To Carolyn's surprise, Dwight shook his head. "I won't lie to you, Corporal. That grenade did a lot of damage to your leg. I think I can save it, but I can't promise you won't have a limp."

Though he winced when Dwight touched a fragment of bone, the young man's face brightened. "You think so?" he asked, almost as if he were afraid to hope.

Without waiting for Dwight's reply, Carolyn smiled at their patient. "Six months from now, you'll be dancing the Castle Gavotte."

As she had hoped, her words distracted him from Dwight's manipulation of shattered bone. "What's that?" he asked. "Me and Molly danced the Turkey Trot back home, but I never heard of no castle dance."

"You mean you haven't heard of Vernon and Irene Castle?" Carolyn thought everyone was familiar with the most famous dancers of the decade. They had started trends in everything from dancing to clothing to hairstyles. In fact, Carolyn's own short hair was modeled on Irene Castle's. "They're Americans," Carolyn explained, "but they got their real start in Paris on their honeymoon."

According to the newsreels, Irene had been wearing her wedding dress when she and Vernon had been asked to dance at one of the most famous clubs in Paris. Hampered by the slim skirt, she could not execute the steps of the popular Turkey Trot or Bear Hug. Instead, she and Vernon had improvised. The resulting dance with its more graceful movements became wildly popular, not only in Paris but across America.

The chloroform was taking effect, and Corporal Seymour's speech was starting to slur. "You don't say."

"I do. You and your Molly will like the Gavotte. I promise."

Dwight continued to examine the leg as Carolyn held it steady. When the corporal flinched again, Carolyn gave him a quick smile. Though by now he should be anesthetized, it appeared he was fighting to stay awake. "I'll make you a deal," she said. "If you go to sleep and trust Doctor Hollins to fix your leg, he and I will dance the Castle Gavotte for you on Christmas Day."

The man's eyes closed. "Deal," he muttered.

For the next half hour, Carolyn handed Dwight instruments, sutures, and bandages, neither of them speaking of anything other than Corporal Seymour's leg. But when the final dressing was applied, Dwight turned to Carolyn. "I'm a doctor, not a dancer," he said, as if the intervening half hour had not occurred and they were continuing the conversation she had had with the patient.

It was hard to read Dwight's mood. Though he did not sound angry, he was not smiling. Of course, Carolyn reminded herself, he rarely smiled, particularly here in the operating room. She bit the inside of her lip, wishing not for the first time that she had thought before she had made the impulsive offer. It was one thing to commit herself, another to make Dwight part of her scheme. Still, a promise was a promise. She would have to convince Dwight to help her deliver this one.

"My granny always said Christmas was a season of miracles."

Dwight nodded, his face as impassive as ever. "It'll take one of those to get me to dance."

He didn't want to do it. That was obvious. But he hadn't refused. Carolyn took comfort from that. "What you need are lessons, not a miracle," she countered.

The suspicion of a smile lit Dwight's face. "Are you proposing to teach me?"

"Of course!" How else was he going to learn? "I love to dance."

"You love dancing; you love shopping. Let me guess. You love Christmas, too."

Carolyn nodded. "Don't you?" Though she had once called him Hollow Heart, Carolyn no longer believed that was true. He was a man who cared deeply about people. It was simply that he saw no reason to display his emotions to the world at large.

Dwight shrugged. "I won't pretend that I'm Scrooge. Normally I like Christmas. It's just that this year . . ."

The sadness on his face made Carolyn think he was remembering happier holidays. Perhaps his nostalgia was because a year ago he had spent Christmas with Louise, while this year they would be apart. To cheer him, Carolyn finished his sentence. "This year you'll be dancing the Castle Gavotte."

"Are you ready?"

Dwight turned, surprised to see Carolyn standing in the doorway of the small room that the hospital staff had turned into a lounge. Before the war, it had been a library, its walls lined with books, its floor covered with a fine Persian rug. Though the shelves remained, the books were gone, sold— or so it was said—to an American millionaire who wanted his newly constructed home to have the trappings of old money, and the rug had been placed in the attic for safe-keeping. But the comfortable leather chairs remained, giving the doctors and nurses a place to seek a few moments of respite.

"Ready for what?" he asked. He hadn't heard the arrival of another convoy of wounded, and Carolyn's expression was playful, not as somber as it would be if she were summoning him to surgery.

"For your first dancing lesson."

The dancing lesson. He had hoped she had been joking when she made the promise to the patient. Even afterwards when she had offered to give him dancing lessons, he had told himself she would forget it. Although why he would think such a thing wasn't clear to Dwight. For all her impulsiveness, Carolyn Wentworth was as determined as he. She reminded him of a terrier he'd once seen—playful as could be, but once he smelled a bone, nothing and no one could distract him until he'd unearthed it.

Dwight wrinkled his nose as he looked at Carolyn. "You're serious about this, aren't you?" Though he phrased it as a question, he knew the answer.

"Indeed, I am. I know you won't let me disappoint Corporal Seymour." Carolyn crooked her index finger. "Come with me, Doctor Hollins. I've found the perfect place for us to dance." Dwight found that hard to believe. There were no perfect places in the hospital and certainly none for dancing.

When she led him into the hallway next to the ambulatory patients' wards, then stopped, Dwight regarded her with misgiving. "Here?" he asked. Though the corridor was empty of stretchers now, it was a public place where anyone could see them. Even worse, the wall that led to the courtyard was lined with long windows, meaning he and Carolyn would be visible to anyone crossing the courtyard.

"It's the only place with enough space," she told him.

There had to be a way out of this. "There's no music," he protested. Dwight knew that the hospital had a Victrola, but he had no intention of telling Carolyn that, not when the absence of music could work in his favor.

"I'll hum." The woman was determined, no doubt about that.

"You're not going to give me a reprieve, are you?"

Carolyn feigned a pout. "You act as if dancing with me would be a horrible fate."

"It's not dancing with you," he explained, remembering the insecurity she had shown when speaking of her siblings. "It's dancing itself that I dread."

Carolyn looked at him as if she could not imagine how anyone would use the word *dancing* in the same sentence as *dread.* "Think of it this way: if you learn to dance, not only will you be able to entertain the patients, but you'll be able to dance with Louise at your wedding."

Dwight frowned. Why did she have to mention Louise? For the past month, he'd been trying not to worry about his future bride. Three days after he had told Carolyn about the missing letters, he had received one from Louise. She had said nothing about not writing, so perhaps Carolyn was right and somehow the letters had been lost in the mail. And yet, though he couldn't pinpoint a problem, Dwight knew there was one. Louise's letters were shorter than before, and there was something almost distant about them. At times he felt that they were letters from a stranger, not the woman he was going to marry. If only this war were over and he were back in the States with Louise!

Dwight looked around. There was no one in sight, no one to watch him make a fool of himself learning the Castle Gavotte. "All right," he told Carolyn. "Let's give it a try."

Though she claimed it was her older sister who was the

teacher, Carolyn appeared to share her sibling's gift for instruction. Dwight felt awkward at first, trying to follow Carolyn's directions. "Put your hand here," she said. "Now, take a step backward." He did, but somehow his foot landed on top of Carolyn's. Though it must have hurt, she simply laughed and said, "Let's try that again." No matter how often he made the wrong move, no matter how often he pinched her toes, she never complained. Instead, she praised him whenever he did manage to step backwards and then sideways, and when at last his feet seemed to be following his brain's directions, she laughed with pleasure.

"That wasn't so hard, was it?"

It was. And yet as she continued to hum and they continued to dance together, what had felt awkward became natural. More than that, it became fun. Dwight had never realized that holding a woman in his arms and gliding across the floor could feel so good. But when Carolyn tilted her face toward his and smiled, those blue eyes sparkling with pleasure, he knew that he could dance with her for the rest of his life.

"Bravo!" a man called.

"Told you, fellas," another crowed.

A third began to hum 'The Wedding March.'

To Dwight's dismay, three soldiers stood in a doorway, their grins telling him they were enjoying his discomfort. The spell was broken.

She shouldn't feel guilty. She wouldn't feel guilty. After all, all they did was dance together. So what if it felt better to dance with Dwight than any of the dozens of partners she had had in the past? So what if dancing with him had made her forget—if only for a few minutes—that they were in the midst of a war? They hadn't done anything wrong. Besides, it wasn't as if they were doing it for themselves; Dwight was learning to dance for the patients.

Carolyn picked up her pen. There was no reason to feel

guilty. And yet . . . Resolutely, she took a piece of stationery from the box and began to write.

Dear Ed,
   How I wish this war were over and we were back in Canela. We'd be dancing with joy.

Frowning, she crumpled the paper and tossed it into the wastebasket. It was a mistake saying they would dance, for Ed had never mastered the art of dancing, no matter how often she had tried to teach him. He wasn't like Dwight, who had learned quickly, despite his claims to the contrary. Carolyn frowned again. She would not, absolutely would not, think about Dwight.

Dear Ed,
   I pray each night that you are safe and that the war will soon end. Wouldn't it be wonderful if the war were over by Christmas? That would make this blessed holiday truly a season of miracles. Be careful, my dear.

Carolyn stared out the window, trying to think of what else to tell Ed. She wouldn't write him about Dwight's dancing lessons. In fact, she would not write anything about Dwight, for Ed's last letter had told her how glad he was that she had found a friend. *If I didn't know you better,* Ed had written, *I might feel jealous of the time you spend with Doctor Hollins, but I do know you, my darling Carolyn, and so I'm thankful that you are able to help him save lives.*

The door swung open, and Helen poked her head inside. "I'm going into town," she said, her grin telling Carolyn that she was feeling better. "Can I convince you to go with me?"

Carolyn nodded and closed her pen. She wished she

knew why it was becoming more difficult to write to Ed. When she had first arrived in France, the words had flowed easily, and she'd enjoyed describing her daily life, trying to infuse even mundane events with humor. But recently she had felt stymied, trying to decide what to say. Oddly, letters to her brother Theo remained easy to compose. With a sigh, Carolyn reached for her cloak. Perhaps a walk into Goudot would clear her mind.

"I need to buy one or two more gifts," she told Helen. Though she had bought everything she had planned, when Carolyn had learned that the Christmas of 1917 was being called "The Christmas That Almost Wasn't," she had decided to buy everyone one more gift, just to show the people in Washington how wrong they were. How foolish could they be? Carolyn couldn't understand why the Council of National Defense had thought that eliminating gift giving could accomplish anything good. She had cringed at the thought of thousands of disappointed children on Christmas morning. Thank goodness the American shopkeepers had managed to convince the Council of its folly.

"Shopping is why I'm going," Helen said. "I want something else for Glen."

As they descended the stairs, Carolyn gave Helen a sideways glance. "I thought the baby was going to be his gift."

"It's the main one," her roommate agreed, "but I want something else."

As they walked into Goudot, their hands thrust into their coat pockets to keep them warm, Carolyn asked Helen about her baby. "When are you going to see a doctor?" Though she knew Helen was reluctant, because she wanted to keep her pregnancy secret for as long as possible, Carolyn was concerned by the severity of Helen's morning sickness. What if something were wrong?

"I'll do it after Christmas," Helen said. "I thought I might ask Doctor Hollins."

Carolyn's step faltered. "Dw . . . er, Doctor Hollins? I thought you were afraid of him?"

Helen's smile reminded Carolyn of a cat she had once seen, grinning over some secret. "That was the old Dr. Hollins. It hasn't escaped my notice—or that of the other nurses—that the man is almost human these days." Helen's brown eyes sparkled with amusement. "And we know who's responsible. We just don't know what you've done to civilize the beast."

Blood rushed to Carolyn's face. "I haven't done anything."

"Of course not." Helen made no effort to hide her sarcasm. "Now, what are you shopping for?"

That was a safe topic, and Carolyn seized it. "I already bought Ed a warm blanket. He keeps complaining that the Army issue is scratchy, so I thought he'd appreciate a new one, but I'd like to give him something more. Maybe something he can eat." For Ed had groused about the sameness of the food, too, telling her that once the war was over, he would refuse to eat another canned tomato.

Rumor was that someone back in the States had decided that canned tomatoes and salmon were highly nutritious substitutes for beef and potatoes and had sent whole shiploads of them to the front lines, much to the soldiers' displeasure. "We want real food," Ed had declared. "None of that monkey meat, either." Monkey meat, Carolyn had learned, was the soldiers' term for corned beef.

As they wandered through the small grocery store, Carolyn stopped and smiled. "Ed will like this," she said, pulling a fruitcake from the shelf. Though Theo had refused to eat their mother's fruitcake, insisting that it was a waste of good rum, Ed had always asked for a second piece. Carolyn had once asked him if he was simply being polite, trying to assuage her mother's feelings, but he had insisted that he found the cake delicious. This one might not have the same flavor as her mother's, but Carolyn hoped it would remind Ed of home and happier times.

She was walking back to the counter when she spied a tin. Stopping to give it a closer look, she grinned. It was perfect.

Though the sun was hiding behind a heavy curtain of clouds, Carolyn felt her spirits rise when she woke on Christmas morning. Perhaps it was foolish to believe that the war had reached its turning point. Perhaps she was being a Pollyanna, thinking that the new year would bring peace. And yet she could not repress her optimism. It was Christmas, and maybe, just maybe, there would be a miracle.

The room felt oddly empty with Helen gone. Though there was no official ceasefire, both sides appeared to have stopped shelling, and so Miss Pierce had given Helen two days' leave to meet Glen. Carolyn missed her roommate's company at the same time that she was happy for her. Dieppe, which was where Helen and Glen planned to spend the holiday, was reputed to be a pretty seaside resort. Carolyn doubted the Guthries would notice much about it other than the fact that they were there together. By now Glen would know that he was to be a father. Carolyn closed her eyes, trying to imagine the man's expression of joy. For Helen and Glen, the prospect of parenthood was nothing less than a miracle, the finest Christmas gift either of them could want.

After she had finished her morning ablutions, Carolyn reached into the armoire and drew out her red silk dress. Though her sisters had laughed when she had packed it, telling her that there would be nowhere to wear anything so fancy, Carolyn had insisted on bringing it and a pair of soft leather dancing shoes. Today she was glad that she had. The color was festive, and the patients would surely enjoy seeing something other than the nurses' somber gray and white uniforms. Even Miss Pierce had agreed that they need not wear their uniforms today. Today was a holiday, and—barring the unexpected resumption of hostilities—it would remain one.

Carolyn fastened the last hook on the dress, then executed a quick pirouette. After months of wearing cotton and wool uniforms, it was wonderful to feel the swirl of silk against her legs. The gown was impractical. There was no doubt of that. The deeply scooped neckline and tiny sleeves were not designed for buildings with a coal shortage, and the fact that she was wearing low pumps rather than her normal high-button boots meant that her ankles were also exposed to the cold. Carolyn didn't care, for there was no denying that her heart felt as light as her feet today.

When she walked into the dining room and saw the garlands draped over the long windows and the candles on the tables, Carolyn was glad she had worn her pretty dress. The kitchen staff had obviously gone to great lengths to make the room beautiful. It was fitting that she was wearing her nicest frock.

Carolyn was even more thankful she had made a special effort when she saw Dwight. His gaze moved slowly from the top of her head to her toes, seeming to assess each inch. And, judging from the gleam that shone in his eyes and the smile that transformed his face, he liked what he saw.

For a second, Carolyn's heart stopped; then it began to race. *Stop it!* she admonished herself. There was no reason to react like a schoolgirl with her first beau. She wasn't a teenager; Dwight wasn't her beau; and she hadn't worn the pretty dress for him. She was simply dressing for the patients. She had promised Corporal Seymour a demonstration of the Castle Gavotte, and the red frock was more appropriate for that than her uniform.

It was good that Dwight liked the dress, but that was merely because his approval confirmed that the men would enjoy seeing her dance the Castle Gavotte. That was the only reason Carolyn's cheeks warmed when Dwight gave a low whistle.

"Very nice," he said. "But aren't you missing something?"

Carolyn shook her head, puzzled.

"Your clothespin." As Dwight grinned, she laughed. She wouldn't classify it as a miracle, but there was no denying that it was pleasant to see Dwight joking.

"I have a whole bag of them," she said softly. Knowing that many of the patients would receive no gifts from home, she had bought a bag of clothespins and written each patient's name on it. It was a silly gift, of course, but that was the point. The clothespins were designed to make the men laugh.

"And not a single one for your nose." Dwight touched the tip of her nose. It was a casual touch, nothing more than the continuation of his joking, and yet the way it made her feel was anything but casual. A shiver of pleasure traveled down her body, and the warmth it generated made her forget that the dining room was cold.

"We'd better eat," she said, trying to pretend that nothing out of the ordinary had occurred. Thank goodness her voice sounded normal! Carolyn wasn't certain how she had managed that, for she most certainly did not feel normal. Fortunately, the room was filling with other doctors and nurses, all seemingly as happy as she that today was a holiday. Their excited chatter defused the tension that had begun to build within Carolyn.

When they finished the light breakfast they had agreed was all they would eat before dancing, she turned to Dwight again. "Are you ready?" Today, instead of his doctor's uniform, he was dressed in a dark suit that emphasized his muscular physique. It was the first time Carolyn had seen him out of his uniform, and she was surprised at what a difference it made. Instead of his jacket with its cargo pockets, metal buttons and standing collar, Dwight wore a normal suit jacket. Though Carolyn suspected the boiled collar and cravat were less comfortable than his uniform, she liked the contrast of the white shirt with the charcoal wool. She also liked the fact that he wore ordinary trousers and shoes instead of military pants bloused into knee-high boots. There might not be a truce, but wearing civilian clothing helped keep the thoughts of war at bay, if only for a few hours.

"Ready?" she asked again.

As Dwight shrugged, the fine wool of his suit moved so smoothly that she realized it must have been custom made for him, not ordered from the Sears catalog the way so many of the suits in Canela were. Carolyn wondered if that had been Louise's influence. She doubted many farmers owned custom suits.

"As ready as I'll ever be." Placing her hand on his arm, Dwight led the way to the ward where Corporal Seymour was recuperating. As they walked along the hallway, Carolyn glimpsed their reflection in the long windows. Out of uniform, their faces wreathed in smiles, they could have been any couple anywhere, out for a brief stroll. It was hard to believe that there was a war only a few miles away.

"Merry Christmas, gentlemen!" Dwight called as they entered the ward. Carolyn made a deep curtsey, pretending she was a debutante in a receiving line. In truth, it wasn't difficult to pretend, for today was such a special day that she could almost convince herself she was back home, planning to dance at the Canela Country Club.

"You came!" A smile lit Corporal Seymour's face.

"Of course we did." Carolyn walked to the injured man's bed and gave him a special smile while Dwight set up the Victrola that he'd found somewhere in the hospital. By some miracle, there was even a platter with music suitable for the gavotte. "A promise is a promise."

Dwight cranked the Victrola. As the music began, he held out his arms, and Carolyn moved into them. They weren't as graceful as Irene and Vernon Castle; Dwight barely missed her toes twice, and she turned a second too early for one of the twirls. And yet, though it was not a flawless performance, Carolyn knew she had never enjoyed a dance more. It felt wonderful being in Dwight's arms, moving with him in time to the music. And when the phonograph wound down and the dance ended, Carolyn wasn't sure what pleased her more, the men's applause or the expression she saw in Dwight's eyes. There was warmth and approval and something else, something she could not identify.

"Can you come back tonight and do it again?" Corporal Seymour asked.

Dwight looked at her, as if waiting for her decision. When she nodded, he said, "Of course," and led her to the next ward.

By the time they had danced for all the patients, Carolyn's feet were more tired than if she had spent a day standing in the operating room, and her cheeks almost ached from smiling. Yet she would not have traded the experience for anything. Christmas was a day for giving, and today more than any Christmas in her memory, Carolyn felt as if she had been blessed with the ability to give. Today she had been more than the decorative Wentworth daughter; she had been useful.

As if he understood what she was thinking, Dwight said, "This hasn't been like any Christmas I've ever spent, and yet . . ." His voice trailed off, and she wondered what he had started to say.

"I loved watching the men's faces. For a few minutes, they looked almost happy." And she had been part of the reason they were happy. How wonderful! Carolyn touched Dwight's arm. "I hope you didn't mind the dancing too much."

He laid his hand on top of hers, and the warmth sent a frisson up her arm. What was it about this man that his lightest touch made her react so strongly? "I hated the idea at first," Dwight admitted, "but now I realize that what I was taught in medical school is true. There's more to healing than setting bones. We need to heal men's spirits, too." His eyes were sober as he looked down at Carolyn. "If jokes and dancing help the men, let's do it more often."

Carolyn's smile was tremulous as she realized that Dwight was telling her he approved of her unconventional methods of dealing with the patients. What a wonderful gift he'd just given her!

By the time Carolyn and Dwight had finished dancing, the kitchen staff was ready to serve dinner. Though they were limited by the shortage of many foods, the cooks had done their best to make the meal a memorable one. Carolyn noticed that today no one complained about the canned tomatoes, because when they were placed next to the spinach, they made the plates look festive. And when the meal was over, the cooks presented each man with a gingerbread star bearing his name. Amidst the caroling and the cheering, Carolyn saw more than one man give his eyes a furtive wipe.

After the men were taken back to their wards, Carolyn and Dwight returned to distribute her clothespins and to dance a second time. If the men had seemed appreciative in the morning, they were more so now, and though her feet ached, Carolyn's heart was light. This was why she had come to France, to make a difference—even if only a tiny one. She said a silent prayer for Ed and Theo and all the other soldiers, hoping that someone was giving them a few moments of happiness today.

When they had returned the Victrola to the storeroom on the third floor, Carolyn turned to Dwight. The storeroom was crowded and dusty, the air musty from dampness and disuse. It was one of the least attractive rooms in the chateau, and yet it was the one place where Carolyn knew they would not be interrupted. Perhaps she should not have been so nervous. After all, the future of the world did not depend on Dwight's reaction. But though Carolyn told herself it wouldn't matter if Dwight didn't like his gift, she did not succeed in convincing herself.

"Merry Christmas," she said, her hands trembling as she pulled the final gift from her bag.

"Merry Christmas, Carolyn," he said at the same moment, handing her a wrapped box.

Carolyn stared at the package, surprised that Dwight, who admitted that he hated shopping, had bought her a gift. "I didn't expect anything," she said. The gift she had chosen for him was a token, designed to ensure that he had at least one package to open. Carolyn wasn't certain whether his family had sent gifts or if he'd asked them not to.

"I hope you like it." There was a note of uncertainty in his voice that touched Carolyn's heart. The man who was so confident in the operating room was just as vulnerable as she.

She unwrapped the box, then gasped as she removed the lid. "I can't accept this." Though the light in the room was dim, there was no mistaking the gleam of gold.

"Don't you like it?" Dwight asked, and again she heard concern in his voice. She didn't want to hurt him, but . . .

"It's beautiful, Dwight." Carolyn looked at him, hoping he'd understand. "I just can't accept anything so expensive. It wouldn't be right." For he had given her the enameled brooch that she had seen in the jewelry store, the one he had been certain Louise would not like. This was a gift for a fiancée or a wife, not an acquaintance.

"Don't tell me your grandmother wouldn't approve," Dwight said with a little smile. "You know I won't believe that."

Carolyn's grandmother would not have approved, nor would her mother, or even her sister Martha. A lady simply did not accept a gift of such value. Flowers, books and candy were acceptable. Anything else put the woman's reputation in jeopardy. Carolyn shook her head. "Granny would not have approved."

But Dwight was clearly not convinced. "I bought this for you, and I want you to have it." Before Carolyn could protest again, he said, "If it eases your conscience or your sense of propriety or whatever it is that's bothering you, why don't you consider it a thank you for all the help you've given me?"

His eyes were shadowed with pain, and Carolyn heard the vulnerability in his voice again. She couldn't hurt him, not on this special day. No matter how inappropriate it was to accept such a valuable gift, she would not refuse it. "This is the most beautiful piece of jewelry I've ever received," she said, pinning the brooch onto her dress. The delicate gold and enamel sparkled against the red silk. Even more importantly, Dwight's eyes sparkled. "Thank you, Dwight." She looked at the box he still held. "I'm afraid your gift is not so magnificent." When she had bought it, she had thought he might like it. Now, she wasn't so certain.

Dwight tore the paper from the box, then laughed when he saw that Carolyn had given him a tin of English toffees. Though Dwight had once mentioned that he liked toffee, the contents were not the reason she had selected the gift. The tin itself was, for it had a picture of a dancing couple painted on its top. When Carolyn had seen it, she had thought of Dwight and their dancing lessons. Though this couple appeared to be more graceful than she and Dwight, when Carolyn looked closely at the painting, it seemed that the man was frowning, as if he were enduring rather than enjoying the dance. Carolyn had laughed in the store and again when she wrapped the gift. She hoped Dwight would laugh when he saw it.

He did. Dwight laughed, and then he laughed again. Reaching forward, he clasped Carolyn's hand. "Oh, Carolyn," he said, his eyes filled with happiness. "You've given me the most wonderful Christmas present I've ever received."

"A tin of toffees?" Though there was no doubting the sincerity of his words, Carolyn couldn't believe that was his favorite gift.

Dwight shook his head. "You might think it's a tin of toffees, but it's more than that." He raised her hand to his lips and pressed a kiss on it. "You've given me the gift of laughter. Thank you, my dear."

Chapter Eight

He didn't mean anything by it. She knew that. The kiss was nothing more than a polite gesture, a type of greeting men used to employ. It had no more significance than his final words had. That had been a casual endearment, a phrase he would have used with any girl, especially on Christmas Day. When he called her "my dear," Dwight meant nothing more than the soldiers did when they addressed Carolyn as "sweetie."

Only a foolish woman would believe that there had been anything more, anything . . . romantic about Dwight's words or his kiss. Carolyn wasn't his dear any more than she was the patients' sweetie. She was simply Nurse Wentworth, who assisted Dr. Hollins in surgery, who had taught him to dance, and who occasionally made him laugh. That was all, and she would do well to remember it.

Carolyn stood at the window, staring into the distance. The rain had turned to snow, and though one of the cooks was predicting that it would change back to rain by morning, Carolyn enjoyed the sparkle of moonlight on the newly fallen snow. It was part of the magic of this special day.

She touched the brooch Dwight had given her, her fingers tingling as they traced the outline of the delicate flowers. She hadn't exaggerated when she had told Dwight that it was the most beautiful piece of jewelry she owned. Reluctantly she unpinned it and placed it back in the box. Though she felt a bit like Cinderella must have when the ball ended, the day was over, and it was time to put her finery away.

As she closed the jewelry box, Carolyn's gaze fell on her left hand, and she felt her cheeks flush. How silly of her to think that the floral brooch was the most beautiful piece of jewelry she owned! Her engagement ring was the most wonderful gift she had ever received. Of course it was. How could she forget the pride and the love that she had seen on Ed's face the day he had slipped it onto her hand? Ed was the most important man in her life; he was the reason she was here in France, and she would do well to remember that too.

But her dreams were troubled, and when she awakened, Carolyn's head ached. If only the war were over. If she were home, surely she would not dream of a brown-haired man who kissed her hand and called her dear.

She was pulling on her stockings when the door opened. "Welcome back!" Carolyn jumped to her feet and hugged Helen as she entered the room. Carolyn was thankful Helen had returned. Maybe now she would be able to think rationally. Terms of endearment, kisses, and pieces of jewelry were subjects almost as dangerous as No Man's Land. She needed to surround them with barbed wire as a reminder to keep her distance.

Helen tossed her valise on the floor and unpinned her hat. "How was your Christmas?" she asked, the satisfied smile on her face telling Carolyn Helen's holiday had been everything she had hoped.

"It was a very pleasant day," Carolyn said. She would not think about Dwight's parting words and gesture or the extravagant gift that was now hidden in a bureau drawer. "The men seemed to enjoy watching us dance." That was what was important, not the parts of the day that she was trying to banish from her memory. Deliberately changing the subject, she asked Helen how Glen had reacted to the news of their impending parenthood.

"He's thrilled!" Helen's face glowed with happiness, and Carolyn felt a twinge of sadness as she wondered whether she would ever be as happy as Helen, secure in her husband's love and the knowledge that they were going to have a baby.

"It seems like a miracle," Helen continued. "We've waited so long, and now all our dreams are coming true. If only this war would end."

Carolyn shook herself mentally, ashamed of her momentary jealousy. Helen and Glen deserved every minute of happiness they could find, and she was a poor friend if she begrudged them even a second of it, simply because she was not so fortunate. She should be thankful that her family's house bore a blue star in one window, the visible reminder that Theo was in the armed forces, and that that star had not been replaced with a gold one. Far too many families had spent this Christmas knowing that gold stars and folded flags would be their final memory of loved ones.

"Did Glen have any news?" Carolyn asked. Though the censors would not let them mention anything in their letters, men at the front sometimes heard about planned offensives or the progress of the war, while the staff in the hospital were among the last to learn what was happening.

When she saw Helen's expression, Carolyn was sorry she had asked the question. "He's worried about something big. There are rumors that Pershing has some secret plan that's going to crush the enemy. But no one knows anything for certain. You know how rumors are." Helen's attempt to smile failed.

"Ninety percent are false."

Though Helen nodded, her lower lip trembled. "I don't

know what I'd do if I lost Glen." She shuddered and closed her eyes. "This war has to end!"

"It will," Carolyn said with more confidence than she felt. In his last letter, Ed had told her that the more cynical of the veteran soldiers believed that the war would never end, that—like the changing seasons—war would be an accepted part of the natural order. A month ago, Carolyn would have said that was unthinkable, but now the unthinkable was being discussed. Surely it would not become reality!

Two weeks later Carolyn was thankful she had not opened her mail in the dining room. Most of the staff and the ambulatory patients were so excited to receive letters that they ripped them open and read them wherever mail was delivered. Carolyn had never done that, preferring instead to take the precious epistles back to her room and savor them in privacy. Normally she chuckled at the stories her sisters recounted, smiled at Ed's tales of his fellow soldiers' attempts to tame the all too common rats, and laughed at Theo's quirky sense of humor. Today she blinked back tears.

Remember how everyone used to laugh at my sixth sense? Theo had written. Carolyn had started to smile, recalling the times when her brother had claimed that intuition told him it would rain or that they would have an unexpected visitor. More times than not, he had been right. But as she scanned the next lines of his letter, Carolyn's smile faded. *Don't tell Martha or Emily. They'll only worry, and there's nothing they can do. The commanders say nothing's planned, but my senses tell me that I'll be in danger soon. It's a bad feeling, Sis. A real bad feeling.*

Carolyn's hands were shaking as she slid the letter back into its envelope. If anyone else had expressed those fears, she might have dismissed them as the natural worries of a man at war. But Theo's premonitions were more difficult to discount. Her palms grew moist and her stomach roiled as she considered what her brother had said. He was right; there was nothing Martha or Emily or even Carolyn herself could do. She wasn't certain why he had confided in her, unless perhaps he thought she would understand, since she was so close to the battlefront. All Carolyn knew was that her own fear was so strong she could taste it.

She began to pace the floor, trying to quell her anxiety, but nothing she did helped. She needed to talk to someone. Helen would understand. She knew exactly what Carolyn was feeling, for she had the same fears for Glen. Helen would listen, Carolyn knew that. But she also knew that she could not burden her friend with her own concerns. That would be unfair.

There was, however, someone else, someone who would help her. Her heart lighter than it had been since she had opened Theo's letter, Carolyn headed for the operating theater. She would try not to think about Theo while they worked; but afterwards she would ask Dwight.

"I hate to bother you." Carolyn waited until they were finished with their patients before she spoke.

Dwight turned from scrubbing his hands and stared at her. Her face must have reflected some of her anguish, for his eyes darkened. "What's wrong?"

"Can we go somewhere less public?" When Dwight nodded, they arranged to meet in the converted library.

"What's wrong?" he repeated when they were in the staff lounge. He had waited until Carolyn had seated herself next to the coal fire, then had dragged a chair so that he sat only a foot from her. Though he did not touch her, his strength seemed to warm her more than the meager fire.

Carolyn swallowed deeply, suddenly unsure whether voicing her fears would strengthen them rather than lessen their power. Though Dwight said nothing, the concern she saw reflected in his eyes made Carolyn realize how much she wanted his advice. Slowly, she began to speak.

"Your brother is right," Dwight said when she finished

explaining what Theo had written. "Worry changes nothing. All it does is weaken us."

She knew that, and yet the knowledge did not reduce the fear. "How do you cope with the knowledge that someone you love may be killed tomorrow? I know I should tell myself that he would be a hero, dying for the cause, but I'm not that strong. Dwight, I don't know what to do."

His eyes darkened again, and this time he laid his hand on top of hers, squeezing it gently. "Fear is like an enemy. If you want to defeat it, you plan a campaign." Carolyn wasn't sure what Dwight meant. He wanted to help her. She knew that. That was why he was holding her hand, why he was giving her his warmth. But a campaign? Carolyn didn't understand the reference. Before she could tell him that, Dwight continued, "What is your greatest fear?"

That was easy. "That Theo will be killed." But as she pronounced the words, Carolyn realized she was mistaken. That was not what she feared most. She shook her head, contradicting her previous declaration. "I'm more worried that he'll be injured and no one will be there to help him." That was the image that sent chills of fear down her spine. Carolyn couldn't bear the thought of Theo suffering and having no one to ease the pain.

"Did your brother ever say that there were no hospitals near him?" Dwight continued his questioning.

"No. He told me there's a field hospital only a few kilometers away." While not as large or well equipped as base hospitals like the one in Goudot, field hospitals were designed to deal with battlefield traumas.

Dwight gave her hand another squeeze. "Think about that when fear strikes again. Tell your enemy he's powerless, because you know that even if Theo is wounded, there are trained doctors and nurses close by to help him. You're here, Carolyn. You know how much good we do. The people at the field hospitals are just as competent. Maybe more so."

Carolyn felt as if the bands that had threatened to squeeze the life from her heart were being eased. "Thank you, Dwight." She managed a weak smile. "I think I'm ready to face the wards now." She wouldn't shirk her duties. Other women were depending on her to help heal their husbands, sons, and brothers. She wouldn't fail them.

When they entered the ward where Corporal Seymour was recuperating, Carolyn handed his chart to Dwight, then watched as he reviewed it and examined the man's leg.

"Have you told your Molly that you're going to dance the gavotte with her?" she asked.

The corporal grinned. "I ain't gonna wait that long. I reckon me and the men are gonna dance at you and the doc's wedding."

As if on cue, the other patients began to hum "The Wedding March." To Carolyn's dismay, she felt her cheeks color. She turned to Dwight, expecting him to deny that there would be a wedding, but instead of the sharp retort she envisioned, he merely shrugged.

"Why didn't you stop them?" she demanded when they were back in the hallway. "I keep telling them that we're not getting married, but they don't listen to me."

Dwight gave her a long, appraising look, as if he were searching her face for something. At last he said, "I learned from a wise woman that laughter heals men's spirits. If the men want to tease us, let them. It doesn't hurt us. We know the truth."

Then why, Carolyn wondered, did the men's humming make her dream of walking down the aisle toward a groom who looked suspiciously like Dwight? It was Ed she was going to marry, Ed Bleeker, the boy next door, the man who had put a diamond on her left hand and promised to love her all his life. Ed was the man she loved.

That night Carolyn wrote Ed a longer letter than normal, telling him the news she had heard from home, regaling him with amusing tales of her patients but neglecting to tell him how the men had graduated from playing Parcheesi to a silly game of humming a ridiculous song. She would not tell him about that, any more than she had told him of Dwight's Christmas gift or his parting words.

Stay safe, my dear, she wrote. As she penned the words, Carolyn wore a triumphant smile. See! The endearment meant nothing special. It was a term to be used between friends. But as she sealed the envelope, she could feel the blood drain from her face. This was Ed! He was more than a friend. Of course he was.

Two days later, Carolyn and Dwight had finished their first shift when the mail arrived. They stood in the far corner of the dining room, letting the others cluster around the mailman. "I hope to hear from Louise today," Dwight said as the mailman began to call out names. "I didn't get a letter from her last week."

Carolyn was surprised. Dwight had told her that she had apparently been right about letters somehow getting lost, because Louise's weekly epistles had resumed. He hadn't mentioned that he had missed another week. Perhaps that was because last week they'd all been discussing President Wilson's Fourteen Points proposal and speculating on whether that would help shorten the war. While the French soldiers whom everyone called *poilous,* focused on the eighth point, that all French territory must be freed, the English and Americans were more concerned with the possibility of a ceasefire. For several days after the president's proposal was made public, the staff had spoken of little else. No wonder Dwight hadn't mentioned Louise's letters.

"That's it," Dwight said, smiling when he received a thick blue envelope. "Louise always uses this color stationery." Impatiently, he tore at the flap. Carolyn was surprised. Normally Dwight was like her and took his mail back to his room to read. He must have been more worried about Louise's silence than he had admitted.

Not wanting to intrude on Dwight's private moment, Carolyn took a few steps away and stared at the mailman, willing him to call her name. When he had emptied his bag but had not called for her, Carolyn looked back at Dwight. To her surprise, his face was ghastly white, his lips clenched tightly. Never before had she seen Dwight look like that. Shocked and more than a bit concerned, she rushed to his side. "I don't believe it," he was muttering when she reached him.

"What's wrong?"

"Nothing." Dwight kept his eyes fixed on the paper that he gripped with his left hand. His right hand was clenched as though he held something.

"You may be a first rate physician, Dwight Hollins, but you're a mighty poor liar." Carolyn tugged on his arm. "Let's go." Whatever was wrong, this was not the place to discuss it. Dwight, she knew, valued his privacy. He would not want his problems overheard.

Though she had expected a protest, he followed as she led the way to the converted library. Deliberately, Carolyn chose the same chair where she had sat the day Dwight had comforted her, and when he started to sit several feet away, she beckoned him closer. Dwight had helped her when she needed a friend; it was her turn to return the favor. She started to reach out, to touch his hand the way he had touched hers, then drew back. A man could do that. It would be unseemly for a woman to initiate such a gesture, even with a friend.

"Tell me what's wrong, Dwight," she said, thankful that no one else was in the library. What had Louise written that had disturbed Dwight so deeply? Was someone in his family ill?

"Please, dear." The word slipped out before she knew what was happening. Thank goodness, Dwight did not seem to notice. "You're worrying me," she added.

Dwight stared at her, the lines that bracketed his mouth

bearing witness to his distress. "It's Louise." He swallowed, his mouth moving as if the simple act were painful. Whatever was wrong with Louise, it was serious.

"Is she ill?" The only thing Carolyn could imagine that would worry Dwight this much was a terminal disease.

In the corner, the grandfather clock chimed the half hour, its bells bright and cheerful, a poignant contrast to Dwight's laugh, which was short and devoid of mirth. "No, she's not ill. Louise is married."

Married? For a second Carolyn did not understand what Dwight was saying. "But she's engaged to you."

He laughed again, and the sound wrenched Carolyn's heart, for Dwight's laughter was not healing. Far from it. "Not any longer," he said. He stared at Carolyn for an instant, and the expression she saw reflected in his eyes wrenched her heart. No one should have to endure pain like that.

"Look," he said and opened his right hand. Carolyn's eyes widened, for nestled in his palm was a ring. That was why the letter had been so thick. Louise had returned Dwight's ring.

"She didn't want me, my ring, or the life we had planned."

At that moment, Carolyn hated Louise. How could anyone be so cruel as to break an engagement when the man was thousands of miles away, embroiled in a war?

Dwight shook his head, as if denying the words he was pronouncing. "I just can't believe it. We had our lives planned so carefully. We both agreed that we were the perfect couple because we had so much in common. And now she . . ."

Carolyn knew that if he left the pain inside, it would fester like the wounds they treated so often. "Did she say whom she married?" Perhaps if she encouraged Dwight to talk, he would be able to lance the wound. Even anger would be preferable to the disillusionment she heard in his voice.

Dwight's face contorted in a grimace. "His name is Harold, and he's the man who's been repairing her automobile."

Carolyn nodded slightly as the pieces to the puzzle began to fit together. No wonder there had been weeks when Louise had not written. No wonder she had told Dwight about the Model T and its frequent repairs. She had apparently been seeing Harold for some time. But Louise and Harold and their romance weren't important. What was important was helping Dwight. The man had been dealt a blow that, even though it wasn't physical, was still serious. Carolyn couldn't let him continue to suffer. There had to be something she could do to cheer him.

"My granny always said—"

Dwight shook his head. "Nice try, Carolyn, but it won't work with me. Remember, I know the truth about your grandmother." His voice was dull and lifeless, the tone telling Carolyn more clearly than the words themselves how deeply Louise's rejection had cut. Dwight was bleeding, and like the soldier Carolyn had seen in the hallway that one morning, he would soon be in shock unless someone stanched the wound.

Carolyn stared out the window, seeking inspiration. All she saw was rain pelting the ground. What could she say? She could try to comfort him the way she had Martha when they'd learned her husband had been killed. Carolyn dismissed that thought when she remembered that the only thing that had seemed to assuage Martha's pain had been when Carolyn had wrapped her arms around her sister. She couldn't do that with Dwight.

What could she say? The truth was, Dwight needed more than words. He needed actions, just as Martha had. "You're right," Carolyn admitted. "There's no point in quoting my grandmother to you. What you need is some of Clothespin Carolyn's wisdom."

A spark of interest seemed to ignite in his eyes. "What do you suggest?"

What indeed? She had spoken impulsively. Now she had to finish a sentence that had no end. Trying to buy herself some time, Carolyn said, "The way to heal a broken heart is to . . ." Perhaps Dwight would think the pause was for drama. The truth was, Carolyn was trying to figure out something that would help him. She stared outside again, and once again all she saw was rain and mud.

If he were going to heal, Dwight had to laugh. He wouldn't laugh on his own. Carolyn knew that, just as she knew that she would have to provoke that laughter. She thought back, trying to remember the times when Dwight had laughed the most. Though he had been amused by some of her antics, the occasions he seemed to find the most pleasure were when they danced. As much as he had protested, each time they had practiced, Dwight had seemed animated and happy.

Carolyn glanced outside again. That was it!

"The way to heal a broken heart," she said firmly, "is to go dancing in the rain."

He stared at her, his eyes wide with disbelief. Surely it wasn't her imagination that the look of despair had faded, even if only slightly. "Have you taken leave of your senses? We'll catch our death of cold out there."

Carolyn felt a bubble of hope begin to grow. He hadn't refused. He was only being cautious. That was very, very good.

"No, we won't," she countered. "Come on." She rose and tugged his hand, refusing to let go. He could have pulled it away; she knew that. But he did not, and that made the bubble expand again. Dwight wanted to be helped; he was going to let her help him.

A feeling of elation swept through Carolyn. It was more

than the satisfaction that came from knowing she was useful. This was different. Somehow, though she couldn't explain why, she felt as if every moment in her life had been leading up to this, and that whatever was happening, it was meant to be. The bubble of hope and happiness filled her. Perhaps it was wrong to feel as if they had crossed a threshold, as if something good were going to come out of today. Perhaps she should still be sharing Dwight's pain. Instead, she felt as if he had been set free.

When they reached the courtyard, Carolyn started to hum the song that had been their practice tune. "Let's dance," she said. Though his face was somber, Dwight drew her into his arms and they began the steps of the Castle Gavotte.

The afternoon was frigid. The Christmas snow had disappeared, turning to cold, sticky mud. Rain was tumbling from the sky, driven sideways by the wind. Within seconds, Carolyn and Dwight were wet. Rain plastered their hair to their heads; mud splashed their legs. The wind howled around them. It was totally absurd to be dancing in the rain. They were cold and wet and this crazy therapy was doing nothing to help Dwight. Though he continued to dance, he said nothing, and his face was unnaturally calm, as though he were deliberately repressing every emotion. Carolyn kept a smile fixed on her face, though inwardly she was crying. If this didn't work, what would she do?

She looked up at Dwight, willing him to see the ludicrousness of their situation. He looked back, steely-eyed. Then he laughed.

Carolyn felt as if her heart had sprouted wings.

"You should see yourself," Dwight said, his lips turning up in the sweetest of smiles.

Carolyn didn't care what she looked like if it made Dwight laugh. She could go through the rest of her life looking like a bedraggled orphan if that was what it took to bring joy to his face.

"Perhaps you aren't aware that this is the height of fashion. Mud encrusted skirts and hair *au naturel* are all the rage in Paris." She kept her voice light, hoping he didn't see how thrilled she was by the sparkle that had returned to his eyes.

Dwight laughed again. "Whatever you call it, you're still the most beautiful woman I've ever seen."

Carolyn stared at him, bemused. This was the second time he had told her she was beautiful, and in both cases, she had sensed no flattery, merely a statement of fact. All her life, people had complimented her on her beauty, but never before had a man seen her looking like a drenched puppy and found her attractive. It was a heady thought. But that wasn't what was important. What mattered was helping Dwight through the day.

"Keep dancing, Doctor Hollins," she said, feigning a stern tone.

"Certainly, Nurse Clothespin."

As she hummed, they continued to dance, laughing as the rain fell and the mud spattered. This was the craziest thing she had ever done, another of the impulsive acts her family had warned her against; and yet Carolyn could not regret a moment of it, for Dwight was laughing, his face more carefree than she had ever seen it.

"We can do better than that," he told her as they completed a glide, stopping shorter than they did on a wooden floor. "Let's try one of those long glides that you taught me."

"Certainly, Doctor Hollins." Carolyn would glide from here to Paris if that made him happy.

When they started the next glide, she took a long step. Afterwards, she wasn't certain whether she had lost her balance or whether it was simply the slippery mud that caused her to slide. All Carolyn knew was that she started to fall. For a second, she was certain she would land face down in the mud in an ignominious ending to what should have been a graceful dance. As she started to tumble forward, strong arms grabbed her, and before she knew what was happening, she was once more upright, held in the circle of Dwight's arms.

Carolyn looked up at him, intending to thank him, but the words died on her lips when she saw the expression in his eyes. Never had a man looked at her with that warmth. Never had a man made her feel as if she were the most precious being on earth. Never had a man's regard caused her heart to skip a beat and then another and then a third.

She wasn't sure how long they stood there, gazing at each other. It might have been a second. It might have been days. Carolyn didn't care. Nothing mattered but Dwight and the wonderful smile she saw in his eyes and on his face. This was what she wanted: to make him happy.

She smiled. He smiled. And then he bent his head, and his lips touched hers. At first it was the lightest of kisses, no more than a feathering of her mouth. But then his embrace tightened, and his kiss deepened, and in that moment the rain and mud disappeared. For a moment in time, the world was perfect, a universe designed for two, a special place where nothing mattered but being in Dwight's arms and feeling his lips on hers. It was magic, pure magic.

Chapter Nine

Carolyn gave a sigh of relief as she opened the door to her room and saw that Helen was not there. Thank goodness! No matter how much she enjoyed her roommate's company, right now she needed time alone. She didn't need to look in a mirror to confirm that her cheeks were flushed, and her hands trembled as she filled the teakettle. Carolyn took a deep breath, willing her heart to stop pounding, then slipped off her shoes and peeled her mud-spattered stockings. If only she could calm her thoughts as easily as she brushed the mud from her skirts. But, though she tried every trick she knew, her mind continued to whirl faster than the merry-go-round she and Emily had ridden until their mother had insisted they'd be ill if they didn't disembark.

When the tea was steeped, Carolyn poured herself a cup, then settled into Helen's rocking chair and took a sip. As the warm liquid dispelled the chill that had permeated her bones, she began to relax. Carolyn closed her eyes and let the memories, as brightly colored as a kaleidoscope, continue to shift, each one bringing a new image. It had been crazy, dancing in the rain. She couldn't deny that. She also could not deny that it had been the single most wonderful

119

event of her life. While she was in Dwight's arms, nothing else had mattered. For a few moments, she had been able to forget the reason they were in France and even the reason she had insisted they dance. For a few moments, they were simply a man and a woman, enjoying each other's company.

Then Dwight had kissed her. The warmth that rose to Carolyn's cheeks owed nothing to the steam rising from the tea. Carolyn stared at the rain that pelted against the windowpanes, remembering. Though other men had kissed her, she had never felt anything like Dwight's kiss. The other kisses had been, at best, pleasant. They had not made her feel as if the world had stopped revolving. They had not caused her to believe she had been transported to a magic place. They had not been warm and comforting at the same time that they had sent shivers down her spine.

Carolyn encircled the cup with her left hand, trying to warm it, and as she did, she heard the soft clink of metal on china. Her ring! Blood drained from her face, and she started to tremble with shock. How could she have forgotten Ed for even a moment? It had been less than an hour since she had condemned Louise for deserting her fiancé. What was wrong with her that she had reacted the way she had? Carolyn bit her lip. Everyone said she was impulsive. She wouldn't deny that that was sometimes true, but she was not irresponsible. Of course she had shivered. What woman wouldn't shiver if she were standing in the rain? As for the strange warmth she had experienced, that had been generated by satisfaction that she had accomplished what she intended: she had helped Dwight forget Louise's rejection, if only for a few minutes.

Carolyn nodded, reassured. It was good to know that there was a perfectly logical explanation for what she had felt, just as there was a perfectly logical reason why Dwight had kissed her. A woman didn't need an advanced degree to find that reason. Dwight was vulnerable, as any man would be when he had been rejected by the woman he intended to marry. Being jilted was like a physical blow; it created wounds. Some men would lash out, trying to cauterize those wounds with anger. But Dwight was a healer. Rather than a harsh cure, he had sought a soothing balm. That was why he had kissed Carolyn. It wasn't that he had any special feelings for her. She had been like the unguent he used on burn victims, a medicine that helped the healing process. She was the salve that he used to prove to himself that at least one woman would not reject him. That was the only reason he had kissed Carolyn.

As for her own reaction, and the way her heart continued to beat faster when she thought of Dwight's embrace, there was a logical reason for that too. It was nothing more than propinquity. Carolyn had heard about shipboard romances, and she had been warned that patients sometimes imagined themselves in love with a nurse simply because they spent so much time together. This was like that. No! Carolyn shook her head so violently that tea splashed onto her saucer. She was wrong, completely wrong. What she felt for Dwight was not and would never be a romance of any kind. It couldn't be. More importantly, she wouldn't let it be, for she did not want to think of Dwight in any romantic context. The reason was simple. Though he might no longer be engaged, she was.

When the war ended, Carolyn was going to marry Ed. They would return to Canela and live happily ever after. In the meantime, Carolyn knew what she had to do. She would not think about Dwight's kiss, and she would make certain that it was never, ever repeated. Surely she could do that.

Carolyn was staring at the wall, wondering why the future seemed so bleak, when she heard footsteps in the hallway. She forced a smile onto her face, hoping it didn't look as artificial as it felt. *Please*, she prayed silently, *don't let anyone have seen us*. Carolyn didn't think she could bear the teasing that was sure to ensue if anyone knew she had kissed Dwight Hollins. The patients had joked about marriage before. They'd be unstoppable if they had seen Carolyn and Dwight's dance and the way it had ended.

Carolyn bit the inside of her lip, reminding herself that she was going to forget that kiss had happened. She needed to start that . . . immediately.

"There you are." Helen's smile looked normal as she hung up her cloak and poured herself a cup of tea. She chatted about her day, not seeming to notice that Carolyn made few replies. Fortunately, Helen said nothing about Carolyn or Dwight or the fact that two crazy people had danced in the rain. Settling in the chair across from Carolyn, Helen reached into her pocket and held out an envelope.

"Was there a second mail call?" Though unusual, it was not unheard of.

Helen shook her head and took a sip of tea. "No. It must have stuck to someone else's letter. I was in the wards when one of the patients asked me to give it to you."

Carolyn smiled as she recognized Ed's handwriting. She would read his letter later, when she was once again alone, and then she would write him a long, newsy letter. Perhaps she would remind him of the time they had crawled under a hedge, thinking it would shelter them from the rain, only to emerge both wet and covered with scratches. That was what she would remember when it rained, Carolyn resolved, not the totally inappropriate embrace that had occurred today.

"You look positively radiant," she told Helen. Though it was true, Carolyn made the comment as much to keep herself from thinking about how she had spent this rainy afternoon as from a desire to compliment her roommate. "Am I right in assuming that the bloom in your cheeks was caused by mail from Glen?"

Helen nodded. "He hasn't seemed this happy since the

war started." She looked down at her stomach. "He told me the baby gives him another reason to stay alive."

"That's important." Carolyn knew all about giving soldiers reasons to be extra careful; after all, that was the reason she had agreed to marry Ed, although she would never tell him or anyone else that. But she didn't want to think about Ed or marriage right now. "How are you feeling?" she asked. Helen's morning sickness seemed to have stopped, and she now had an insatiable appetite.

"I'm feeling fat." Helen patted her stomach.

"You don't look fat." Though her uniforms were a bit tighter than they had been a month ago, Helen's increasing girth was barely noticeable.

"It won't be long now before my condition is obvious." Helen opened a tin of shortbread and offered Carolyn a piece. "You've heard about mixed blessings, haven't you?" she asked. "The baby is one of them. I'm excited about being a mother, but I don't want to leave here. Does that sound odd—someone who doesn't want to leave a war zone?" Helen wrinkled her nose as if in disgust over her own ambivalence. "The problem is," she said, her words more clipped than usual, "going back to England means that I'll be further from Glen. Besides, I'll miss you."

"I'll miss you, too." Carolyn doubted any other roommate would be as congenial as Helen. She had been fortunate, sharing a room with Helen.

"When the war is over, you and Ed will have to visit us."

Though Carolyn nodded, she had difficulty imaging herself and Ed at the Guthries' home. Helen had described it in such detail that Carolyn could picture herself there. She could even imagine herself walking through the boxwood maze, a man at her side. The difficulty arose when she looked at the man and realized he wasn't her fiancé. He looked like . . . No! She wouldn't think about *him*.

When Helen had taken the dishes to the bathroom to

rinse them, Carolyn opened Ed's letter. Today more than ever she needed the reminders of home and why she had come to France that Ed's letters always brought. Carolyn slid the paper from the envelope. She had read only a few paragraphs when she felt the blood drain from her face. No! It couldn't be. Carolyn forced herself to reread Ed's words. She had not imagined them.

Is something wrong? he had written. Oh, yes, so much was wrong, but he wasn't supposed to know that. *Perhaps it's my imagination that your last letters have sounded different, but I'm worried.* Carolyn flinched as if she had been struck. She had failed in her most important undertaking. It appeared that even though she had tried to make her letters seem carefree, somehow Ed had realized that she was concealing something. Instead of reassuring him, she had caused him worry. Carolyn closed her eyes and took a deep breath. She would make it up to him, starting today. Ed was going to get the most cheerful letters of anyone on the Western Front.

When she had gotten her heartbeat back to normal, Carolyn returned to Ed's letter. *I love you so much, my darling.* The words were there in black and white. *And I love you,* she thought. She would tell him that each time she wrote. Ed must never doubt her love.

As Carolyn turned the page and read his final words, tears filled her eyes. *All I want is for you to be happy. Remember that, if something should happen to me.* She dashed the tears from her cheeks, and her hands trembled as she slipped the letter back into the envelope. Unlike Theo, Ed had never spoken of the possibility of injury or death. Why, oh why, had he raised that specter now? Was it something she had said or—just as bad—something she had not said? Willing her hands to be steady, Carolyn reached for a piece of stationery.

My dearest Ed,
   You always were too perceptive, and as usual

you've found me out. I thought I was hiding it, but it seems I was unsuccessful, and you've unmasked me. Yes, something is wrong, though I'm ashamed to admit it, lest everyone nod their heads and say, 'What else would you expect from Carolyn Wentworth? She always was the frivolous daughter.' The truth is, this constant rain has worn me down ...

Carolyn stared at the paper, hoping Ed would believe her lies. He had to; he simply had to.

Dwight was whistling as he soaped his face. Had there ever been such a glorious day? He grinned as he looked into the mirror, carefully wielding the razor. By all rights, he should be dejected. Louise had jilted him, and his life plan was in shambles. Instead, he felt relieved, as if a burden had been lifted. He hadn't felt that way last night. After he'd left Carolyn, the euphoria that that crazy dance and that even crazier kiss had created had dissipated, and he had found himself overcome with anger. It was a phenomenon he had observed in some of his patients' families when a loved one died. At first they would be in shock, doing and saying things that often seemed irrational. But shock would fade, replaced by a fierce anger. In that state, they would lash out at almost anyone.

Fortunately for Dwight's roommates, no one had been in the room when he had hurled the ring Louise refused to wear. How could she do this to him? Dwight had bent down, picking up the ring and clenching it so tightly that the stone had cut his hand, while he dealt with his fury. It was unconscionable that Louise would break their engagement, but it was even worse that she had been seeing Harold for many months and had never told Dwight that she was having second thoughts about their engagement. How dare she deceive him?

His anger had raged, and he had been certain he would

be unable to sleep. Inexplicably, once he had fallen asleep, he had slept well—and dreamlessly—and had wakened with an unexpected sense of relief. The odd thing was, Dwight hadn't been aware of carrying a weight. Oh, he'd known that his responsibility to the injured soldiers weighed on him. That was to be expected. But he hadn't realized that the thought of marriage had been like a yoke. It was only now that it was gone that he felt oddly carefree. Perhaps he was not meant to marry.

Dwight flicked soap into the bowl, then stropped the razor. The way he was feeling made no sense, just as it made no sense that he was thinking of Carolyn and the kiss they had shared. Admittedly, it had been the best kiss of his life. Dwight grinned at the sheer absurdity of it. No one would believe that he, solemn Dwight Hollins, had gone dancing in a muddy courtyard, with rain drenching him and wind whistling through his clothing. Even more incredible was the fact that he had actually enjoyed the dance and that he had somehow wound up kissing his partner, the beautiful and oh so kissable Clothespin Carolyn.

Dwight grinned again. Though he spent hours with Carolyn every day, until yesterday he had not realized just how kissable her lips were. Even though he had danced with her countless times when they were practicing for their Christmas exhibition, he had never realized how wonderful it would feel, holding her close to him, or how her smile would heal the lacerations Louise had inflicted. The fact was, Carolyn was a special woman, and yesterday had been a special day. Dwight rinsed and dried his face, then resumed his whistling.

She didn't look any different, he realized as Carolyn took her place opposite him in the operating theater. Her uniform looked the same as always, and she worked with the same precision she always did. She even greeted him with the same smile she always wore. Why, then, did he think that today was different? Surely it wasn't only that the weight was gone."

"Suture." He held out his hand, waiting for her to place the thread in it. When she did, her fingertips brushed his and Dwight almost dropped the suture. Had she experienced it, that electrical current that had swept through him? It had felt a bit like the time he had inadvertently touched a bare wire with wet hands. There was the same shock; and yet the similarity ended there. For whereas touching the wire had been unpleasant, the touch of Carolyn's fingers on his was exciting and made him crave more.

Dwight clenched his jaw. This was absurd. He was in an operating room where men's lives depended on his skills. They needed his total concentration. He could not afford to be distracted, thinking of how beautiful Carolyn was or how sweet her lips had tasted. After all, he was a grown man, not a moonstruck youth.

"Forceps." This time Dwight was careful to grab the instrument by the very end, as far from Carolyn's fingers as was humanly possible. There! He was once more on an even keel. The little shock had been a momentary aberration, nothing more.

The rest of surgery was uneventful, as he and Carolyn worked to bind wounds and stave off infections. It was amazing, Dwight realized, how well they worked together. It was almost as if they choreographed their steps as carefully as the Castles, those dancers she kept talking about, did. Except for that one moment when he had reacted so oddly to her touch, they had functioned as a team, moving with precision, never faltering. It was, other doctors had told him, something they had never before seen. When he had first heard one of his colleagues' comments, Dwight had wondered what had caused the difference. Now he knew. It was Carolyn. She was special.

"Are you ready for dinner?" he asked her when they were scrubbing their hands at the end of the day. Though he had tried to keep the thoughts at bay while they worked, there was no longer any reason to deny that he had been looking forward to spending some time with Carolyn. Her gentle humor would keep him laughing. Carolyn had told him that laughter healed. After yesterday and the way laughter had turned into something wonderful, something that healed him in ways he had never even dreamed possible, he now knew he wanted to laugh every day.

But Carolyn, it seemed, did not agree. She shook her head slowly. "I promised to visit Corporal Seymour," she said.

Dwight raised an eyebrow. There was no reason she had to go to the wards now. "I stopped by this morning," he told her. "The corporal is doing well."

Though she nodded in acknowledgment of his assurance, it was clear that Carolyn was determined to make the visit now. And though she said nothing more, Dwight sensed that she was unwilling to dine with him today. It was, he tried to tell himself, understandable. After all, yesterday had been an extraordinary day for both of them. Perhaps she needed time to adjust to all that had happened.

"Would you like to join me on my rounds?" he asked when they had finished their shift in the operating theater the next day.

Carolyn gave him a little smile as she shook her head. "I need to write Ed a letter," she said.

Ed. Of course. Dwight tried to quell his disappointment that writing a letter was more important than being with him . . . and the patients, of course. It was foolish to wish Carolyn were free. After all, it wasn't as if Dwight wanted to marry her himself. Carolyn wouldn't be the perfect doctor's wife the way Louise would have been. Carolyn was too much of a distraction, and her impulsive actions would undoubtedly cause problems. Dwight was a man who liked his life neatly arranged; Carolyn would wreak havoc with that arrangement.

He knew that. But knowing that Carolyn was engaged to another man and that, even if she were not, she was not the woman for him, didn't stop his mind from moving in unexpected directions. He thought about her during the day, and even sleep provided no respite from his fantasies. Last night he had dreamed of a woman coming out of a pleasant house. Though he had never seen the house before, somehow Dwight had known that it was his house, the one he had bought for his family. And when he woke, he realized that it was Carolyn he had seen leaving the house, her backward glance telling him that she lived there, too. It was foolish, of course, to have dreams like that, for they could never come true. Nevertheless, Dwight could not deny that he had awakened with a smile on his face after he had dreamed of sharing his life with Carolyn.

The sun was shining the next morning. It was, Dwight told himself, a good omen. Though she might dance in the rain, Carolyn loved sunshine. Surely she would agree to accompany him when he walked into Goudot. But she did not, and this time the reason she gave sounded like a feeble excuse.

It was not his imagination. The first two days, he had thought it merely coincidence that he and Carolyn were not in the dining room or the staff lounge at the same time. Now he knew that it was a deliberate move on her part. She was avoiding him. She could not avoid him in the operating theater, but she could—and did—ensure that they did not meet anywhere else.

Dwight frowned as he realized there was only one reason for her changed behavior. The kiss. It was as clear as today's sky that she regretted it. He ought to regret it, too. After all, she was engaged to Ed. He had no business kissing another man's fiancée. But, try though he might, Dwight could not regret the sweetest moment of his life.

* * *

Dwight was back from his excursion into Goudot. Carolyn made certain of that before she grabbed her cloak. The last thing she wanted to do was inadvertently meet him, when what she needed to do was to distance herself from him. It was supposed to be getting easier. By now she should have been able to relegate that one afternoon to its proper place, a tiny spot buried deep inside her memory. Carolyn had heard that memories faded with time. Unfortunately, try though she might to ignore it, this one wouldn't be banished.

The rain that had stopped for a few hours began again, and that only made it worse. Though Carolyn had once dreaded rain, now she could not help smiling when it came, for the sight of rain triggered memories that she could not dismiss. Rain reminded her of Dwight. More than that, it reminded her of that magic afternoon when they had danced in the rain. The worst part was, she didn't need rain to bring that scene to the forefront of her mind. No, indeed. Each night she dreamed of Dwight and how wonderful it had felt to be held in his arms. Each night, they were dancing. And each night she relived the kiss they had shared. It was wrong. Carolyn knew that. She was engaged to Ed. She loved Ed, and Dwight was . . . just a friend.

Carolyn furled her umbrella and shook it before she entered the candy store. She had come into town to buy something for Ed. Though she had tried her best to make her correspondence cheerful, his last letters had seemed so filled with foreboding that she wanted to do something special to help boost his spirits.

"I'll take some of that." Carolyn pointed to a tray of licorice. When she mailed it to Ed, she would remind him of how they used to sneak pieces from his mother's candy jar, forgetting that—unless they were very careful—they would have sticky residue on their fingers and mouths that would betray their theft. Ed would laugh. At least she hoped he would.

As she paid for the candy, Carolyn spotted the display of tinned toffees. Though she had worried about his reaction, Dwight had been visibly pleased by the gift. How he had laughed when he'd seen the dancing couple on the lid! Carolyn smiled at the memory, then bit her lip. Thinking of Dwight was like a disease, and no matter what she did, she seemed unable to find the antidote. She had to! Somehow she had to stop the memories. It wasn't right that everything she saw or did reminded her of times she and Dwight had spent together. She couldn't continue to live this way, torn between her traitorous memory and her sense of honor.

When she returned to the hospital, Carolyn went to the wards. Though she no longer performed any of the aides' functions, she enjoyed visiting the men. Sometimes she would write letters for them, but most often she would find three who would play a game of Parcheesi with her. For men like Corporal Seymour who were confined to their beds, the game seemed to provide a welcome respite from staring at the ceiling.

"Where's the doc?" Corporal Seymour asked as Carolyn opened the Parcheesi board and pulled out the markers.

"Yeah," the man in the next bed chimed in. "We don't see him with you any more."

Carolyn kept a smile fixed on her face. There was no point in telling the men that she was deliberately distancing herself from Dwight, that that was the only hope she had of ending those all too disturbing dreams. "Our schedules are different now," she said as calmly as she could. Thank goodness her voice did not quaver. Carolyn knew her cheeks were flushed, but perhaps the men would not notice. It was annoying that the mere thought of Dwight made her heart flutter and brought a flush to her face.

Corporal Seymour shook his head as if he recognized the lie. "C'mon, Nurse Carolyn. You can't fool us. I reckon you and the doc had a lovers' spat." A lovers' spat! Carolyn's face felt so hot that she was certain it was as bright as a strawberry. A lovers' spat, indeed! Preposterous!

Though Carolyn said nothing, Corporal Seymour adopted a stern expression. "Take my advice. You better kiss and make up."

Kiss Dwight? That was the last thing Carolyn would do. Once was enough. Once was more than enough. Carolyn glared at the men. She thought they were her friends; instead, they had turned into tormentors, teasing her with images of things that could never be.

When Carolyn remained silent, the second patient chuckled. " 'Course," he said, "if you're lookin' for a new fella, I'd be mighty glad to volunteer my services."

This conversation had gone on too long. Carolyn handed the dice to the corporal, hoping he'd take the hint and start playing. Instead, he turned to his partner, "Shucks, Fred. We ain't got a chance. Can't you see she's still wearing that ring?"

Though she had hoped that the men would tire of the subject, it seemed that they needed to be reminded of the true situation. "I've told you that I'm engaged to a soldier. He's from my hometown, and his name is Ed."

"Does Ed know how you and the doc moon over each other?"

Carolyn shook her head in denial. "Dr. Hollins and I are friends. That's all." Of course it was.

The man named Fred gave her a piercing look. "Didn't your granny tell you it was wrong to lie? C'mon, Nurse Carolyn. We may be wounded, but we ain't blind."

Carolyn stared at the two men, horrified. It had been one thing when they had hummed "The Wedding March." Though that had bothered her more than it had Dwight, she had still thought it harmless entertainment. But that had been before. Before the dance. Before the kiss. Before the dreams. Now, it appeared, the situation was out of control.

She couldn't deny that she thought of Dwight far too

often. She didn't moon over him the way Corporal Seymour claimed. Of course she didn't. But she couldn't deny that Dwight played a starring role in her dreams and her thoughts. If that was obvious to the men, who else had seen it? The staff? Carolyn shuddered. Then, as an even more frightening thought crossed her mind, she could feel the blood drain from her face. Did Dwight know? Carolyn shuddered again, then straightened her shoulders. She knew what she had to do. No matter how painful it might be, she could not let the situation continue.

"Are you certain, Carolyn?" Miss Pierce leaned across the desk, her expression indicating that she did not approve of Carolyn's suggestion.

"Yes." Though it might appear impulsive, Carolyn knew there was no alternative. When she had heard the soldiers talking, she had realized there was only one possible course of action. "I'm worried about my fiancé and my brother," she said, rationalizing the decision she had made. "I want to be closer to them."

The head nurse pursed her lips. "Are you sure that's the only reason?"

Carolyn's eyes widened. There was something in Miss Pierce's tone that told Carolyn she knew that being closer to Ed and Theo was an excuse. If Carolyn had had any doubts, Miss Pierce's reaction would have squashed them. If her feelings were so obvious, Carolyn had no choice. She had to leave. She had to put a physical distance between herself and the reason for those traitorous thoughts.

"Yes," she lied. "That's the reason."

Miss Pierce was silent for a long moment, staring at her steepled fingers. Then she raised her gaze to Carolyn's and nodded. "If you're certain that you want to leave, I'll approve your transfer to a field hospital." Miss Pierce's eyes were solemn. "I won't deny that we'll miss you here. You've done what no other nurse was able to do, which is to satisfy Doctor Hollins. I appreciate that more than you'll ever know, but I won't stand in your way if you feel you can serve the men better at the front."

"I do." They were only two words, a simple response to Miss Pierce's question. But as she heard herself pronouncing them, Carolyn's mind transported her to a far different setting. For a second, she was no longer in the head nurse's office. Instead Carolyn pictured herself in a church, her hand clasped in Dwight's as she repeated those words in a very different context. Carolyn clenched her fists in frustration at the direction her thoughts had taken. There was no doubt about it. She had to leave.

"The transfer may take a few weeks," Miss Pierce told her. "Until it comes through, you can always change your mind."

"I won't." *I can't!*

Chapter Ten

"I don't believe you." Helen looked up from her knitting, her brown eyes widening in surprise as Carolyn told her of her conversation with Miss Pierce. Helen had been ensconced in the rocking chair, her knitting needles clicking rhythmically, when Carolyn returned to their room. Though she still had told no one of her pregnancy and could not knit in the common rooms, lest someone guess her secret, Helen spent most evenings working on a layette.

"It's true. I asked for a transfer to a field hospital." Carolyn wrapped her arms around her middle, trying to stop the shivers that were wracking her body. A moment ago, she had felt as if she were burning with fever; now she was chilled. It must be something she had eaten. This odd feeling couldn't possibly be the result of the decision she had made. There was no doubt she was doing the right—and the only—thing she could to cure the illness that had been plaguing her.

Laying down the tiny baby sweater that she was knitting, Helen stared at Carolyn. "You misunderstood me. I believe that you asked for the transfer. What I don't believe is your reason."

"That's simple." And it was, though that reason made

135

Carolyn shiver again. "I'm worried about my brother and Ed. I want to be closer to the front in case something . . ." Her voice caught on the words, and she swallowed deeply before she said, "in case something happens to either of them."

Though Carolyn hadn't wanted to tell Helen her fears because Glen was also serving in the trenches, she worried about both Theo and Ed. Theo hadn't repeated his fears about being in a bad situation, but his last few letters had seemed strained, as if he were concealing something. And Ed. Carolyn bit the inside of her cheek to keep from crying. She was afraid of what Ed might do.

I know I'm a hero to you, he had written, *but I don't feel like a hero. Carolyn, my dear, I want to do something to make a difference in this terrible war.*

When she had received the letter, Carolyn had been horrified. *No!* she had shrieked. She had reached for a piece of paper, intending to write to Ed, imploring him not to do anything foolish. But before she could begin, a convoy of wounded had arrived, and she—like the rest of the staff—had spent the next three days working almost around the clock. By the time she was able to write to Ed, four days had passed.

"I'm worried about Ed and Theo," she repeated.

"That's what you say." Helen's expression reminded Carolyn of her mother's when she had caught one of the children in a lie. Like Mama, Helen appeared disappointed and faintly hurt.

"It's the truth," Carolyn insisted. Admittedly, it was only part of the truth, but Helen didn't need to know that. The fact was, she was worried because she had not heard from either Theo or Ed, and the reports from the front indicated that fighting was heavy.

Her roommate shook her head. "It's bad enough that you're lying to me. Don't make it worse by lying to yourself."

"What do you mean?" Carolyn shuddered again. Was it possible that everyone in the hospital knew of her traitorous thoughts and dreams about Dwight? She shouldn't have been surprised. Though Helen had never said anything, if Miss Pierce and the patients believed Carolyn was, to use Corporal Seymour's words, mooning over Dwight, it was likely Helen had also guessed that Carolyn thought of Dwight far too often. That was one of the problems with the hospital. They all spent so much time together that there were few secrets.

Helen picked up her knitting and studied it for a moment before she looked up again. When her gaze met Carolyn's, her eyes were serious. "It's obvious to me that you're in love with Dwight."

In love! This was worse than being accused of mooning over him. The blood drained from Carolyn's face, then rushed back again. "That's not true," she insisted. "Dwight is a friend."

Helen raised an eyebrow. When she spoke, her clipped accent was more pronounced than normal, a sign of how deeply she felt. "You can tell me whatever you want, but in your heart, you know the truth."

"The truth is that I love Ed." Even to her own ears, Carolyn's protest sounded weak.

Surprisingly, Helen did not appear to disagree, for she nodded. "I don't doubt that."

She probably should have let the subject die, but Carolyn could not, not when Helen had accused her of self-delusion. "If you believe that I love Ed, why are you insisting that I'm in love with Dwight?"

Helen slipped three stitches to a holder. It was only when she had completed the cable that she raised her eyes to meet Carolyn's gaze. "As you said before, it's simple. Loving someone and being in love with him are different."

"What exactly do you mean?" Her sister Martha had spoken of being in love, but she had never made a distinction between love and being in love. Carolyn wanted to hear her friend's explanation, for if there was ever a woman who was in love, it was Helen. Her face sparkled and her voice took on a special timbre whenever she spoke of Glen. Not even when she was a newlywed had Martha looked like that.

Helen finished the row of stitches, as if she were in no rush to answer Carolyn's question. "When you love someone," she said, "you want them to be happy. You'll do whatever you can to make them happy."

"You're right. That's how I feel about Ed." Carolyn wanted him to be safe and happy; that was why she had agreed to marry him; that was why she had come to France.

Helen nodded as if she had expected Carolyn's response. "I would venture to say that what we've just described is also the way you feel about Theo."

Carolyn was silent for a moment, considering Helen's theory. She wanted to deny it, but she wouldn't lie. "That's true," Carolyn said, not liking the direction the conversation had taken. "But I'm not going to marry Theo."

Helen reached forward and patted Carolyn's hand. "If you're wise, you won't marry Ed, either."

That was not what Carolyn wanted to hear. "But I love Ed," she protested.

"And you're in love with Dwight." Helen held up a hand. "Don't interrupt. I want you to hear what I have to say." She took a deep breath, then exhaled slowly, and Carolyn guessed she was searching for the right words. "Being in love is not the same as loving someone," Helen said. "I imagine it's different for everyone, but for me it's as if Glen is part of me—the way an arm or a leg is, only more so. Without him, I feel as if I'm only half a person. I need him to make me complete." Helen leaned forward again, her eyes pleading with Carolyn for understanding. "That isn't to say that I can't be happy when Glen is not with me. I can, but I always feel as if I'm missing something."

Carolyn watched Helen's lips curve in the sweetest of smiles as she thought of her husband.

"I don't feel that way about Dwight," Carolyn said firmly.

Helen raised an eyebrow. "Don't you?"

There she was! Dwight's pulse began to race as he recognized Carolyn's figure. She was crossing the courtyard and appeared to be heading for the laundry. If he hurried, he could catch her before she had a chance to invent an excuse not to talk to him.

"Carolyn!"

She turned, and he saw that her cheeks were flushed as if she had a fever. Perhaps she was ill. Perhaps that was the reason for her odd behavior. Perhaps it had nothing to do with the kiss they had shared. Though he didn't want Carolyn to be ill, Dwight couldn't deny the surge of hope that raced through him at the thought that there might be a logical reason for both Carolyn's apparent avoidance of him and the story he had heard.

"Hello, Dwight." He took comfort from the fact that she remembered his first name. Since she had refused to see him outside of the operating theater, he had not heard his name on her lips in days, and he had missed that. That and so much else. The camaraderie, the confidences, the laughter, even the dancing. Especially the dancing, for how could he forget the last time they had danced?

"I thought you were on your rounds." Her color remained high, and her voice was so devoid of inflection that he began a mental catalog of what might ail her. It wasn't a fever, for her eyes were not glassy. But something, it was clear, was amiss.

"I was on my rounds," he admitted, not wanting to think of the patients' reaction when he bolted from the ward or the fact that he was not properly dressed for a February afternoon. He had been in such a hurry to see Carolyn that he hadn't bothered to put on a coat. "I need to talk to you."

The unnatural color drained from her cheeks, and she lowered her gaze, as if she found the muddy courtyard fascinating. That wasn't like Carolyn, but then nothing that had happened recently had been like the Carolyn he used to know. "Talk about what?" she asked.

There were a dozen things Dwight wanted to discuss, but one outweighed the others. "I heard a rumor, and I wondered if it was true."

Though he would not have thought it possible, her pallor increased. She was obviously uneasy, and that wasn't like Carolyn any more than staring at the ground was. More than anyone Dwight knew, she was self-confident. He knew from the stories she had shared with him that even when she was unsure of herself, she put on a brave front, convincing others that she was carefree Carolyn. Today was different. This was not the Carolyn who had worn a clothespin and danced in the rain.

She shrugged her shoulders but failed to meet his gaze. "I guess it depends on the rumor. You know most are pure fiction." Though she managed a laugh, it was so devoid of mirth that it failed to reassure him. A gust of wind tugged at Carolyn's cap and blew through Dwight's shirt, chilling him almost as much as Carolyn's forced laughter.

"I heard you asked for a transfer." It was amazing how much it hurt even to pronounce the words. When he had heard the rumor, Dwight had been shocked by the depth of the pain he had felt. He and Carolyn were friends; he was certain of that. Why, then, hadn't she discussed her plans with him? Surely that was something friends did. Surely whatever it was that had made her seem so distant recently wasn't serious enough to keep her from telling him she was leaving Goudot.

Carolyn clenched her hands in a nervous gesture he had never before seen. "That rumor is true," she said quietly.

"Why?" Dwight demanded. Though she had spoken softly, his question came out with more force than he had intended. "Don't you like working with me?" That was one of the fears that had haunted his days, that and the fear that he had destroyed their friendship by kissing her. Perhaps he should apologize for the kiss, but it would be a lie to say that he regretted it. He didn't regret the kiss. How could he, when it was the brightest spot in his life since he had come to France? If he were being totally honest, he would admit that the kiss he and Carolyn had shared was the brightest spot in his life. Period. How could he regret that? What he regretted was the loss of the camaraderie he and Carolyn used to share.

Shaking her head, she said, "It's not that I don't like working with you. I'm worried about Theo and Ed." Though the words sounded sincere, Carolyn refused to meet his gaze, making Dwight wonder if there was more to her decision than the reason she had given. "I want to be closer to them," she added.

Another gust of wind reminded Dwight that he was not dressed for the weather. He would have encouraged Carolyn to go inside, but now that she was finally talking, he didn't want to do anything that might stop the flow of conversation. "I thought you were comfortable with your brother's situation. Did something happen that I don't know about?" That hurt, too. She had come to him the day she had received Theo's letter with its premonition of danger. If there was more disturbing news, why hadn't she shared it with him?

This time Carolyn raised her eyes to meet his. "Ed's last letters worry me. I want to do whatever I can for him."

Dwight swallowed deeply. Ed. Of course. That was what made the difference. That was why Carolyn had behaved so out of character recently. She was worried about Ed. Dwight couldn't even chide her for not confiding in him when he himself hadn't told Carolyn his worries about Louise until she had pried them from him.

Dwight nodded, acknowledging Carolyn's words and agreeing that her decision was right. He was being selfish, wanting her to stay here, to help him in surgery, to brighten his days. Carolyn was promised to another man. Of course her first loyalty had to be to Ed. Of course she had to do whatever she could to keep her future husband safe. It was only Dwight's foolishness that made him wish someone cared for him the way Carolyn did for Ed. Ed Bleeker was a lucky man.

"Is there anything I can do to help you?" After all the assistance she had given him, the least Dwight could do was offer to help her.

"No." Carolyn's lovely blue eyes filled with pain. "This is something only I can do."

He understood that. He might not like the thought of Carolyn's leaving or the fact that she would be in more danger closer to the front, but he understood that this was something she had to do alone. "Just remember that I'm your friend." Oh, how he hoped she still viewed him in that light! "If you ever need me, all you have to do is ask."

Carolyn gave him a long, appraising look. "Thanks," she said at last. It was a single word, but the tone told Dwight that she would never ask. The magic they had once shared was gone.

"Carolyn, I have a letter for you." The mailman handed her an envelope as he distributed letters in the dining room. Carolyn reached for it eagerly, hoping it was from either Theo or Ed, but the handwriting was one she did not recognize. Judging from the script, the author was a man. Carolyn thought quickly. It had been two weeks since Dwight had spoken to her in the courtyard, two weeks and two days since she had requested her transfer. Perhaps the letter was her new orders. Then she realized that those would come through Miss Pierce. Why was a strange man writing to her?

Curious, Carolyn hurried back to her room. No matter how the other residents would open their mail in the common areas, sharing tidbits with anyone who would listen, she preferred her privacy. Normally she would brew a pot of tea and settle into the rocking chair to read her letters. Today she waited only until she was inside her room to slit the envelope. As her eyes scanned the single sheet of paper, Carolyn felt the blood drain from her face. Stunned, she gripped the back of the chair, then sank heavily onto her bed.

It can't be true! Please, God, don't let it be true! But as she read the words for a second and then a third time, Carolyn knew this was not a nightmare from which she would awaken. This was real. Ed was dead. A member of his company had written, knowing that the official notification would go to Ed's mother and that it might be several weeks before Carolyn heard the news. Ed, the stranger wrote, had volunteered to go behind enemy lines and had been killed by a grenade. But before he had died, Ed had destroyed a critical radio tower. He was a hero. *No!* Carolyn cried. *I didn't want you to be a hero! I wanted you to be safe.*

As the tears streamed down Carolyn's face, she folded the letter and replaced it in the envelope, and as she did, she realized that the stranger had sent something else. Carolyn stared at the unopened letter. She didn't need to read it to know what it said. This was the letter she had written to Ed, begging him to stay safe, the letter that had been delayed because of the influx of wounded. Ed had not received it, and so he had volunteered for a dangerous mission.

Would he have acted any differently if he had read her letter? Carolyn didn't know. All she knew was that she had failed Ed. She had agreed to marry him. She had come to

France to be near him. She had done both of those things
to keep him alive, but they hadn't been enough. She had
failed Ed, and in failing him, she had failed herself.

As sobs wracked her body, Carolyn curled into a ball on
her bed and wept for the loss of her friend and the dreams
that would never come true. She wept for Ed's mother, who
would replace the blue star in her window with a gold one.
But most of all she wept for Ed, whose life had ended much
too soon.

Carolyn wasn't sure how long she lay there. She was
vaguely aware that the sun had set. How fitting that she
was in the darkness. When she heard footsteps and the door
opened, she buried her head in the pillow.

"What's wrong?" When Carolyn said nothing, Helen
switched on the light, then ran to Carolyn's side. Wrapping
her arms around her, she repeated her question.

Reluctantly Carolyn struggled to a sitting position. "Ed's
dead." It was the first time she had said the words aloud,
and the simple act of speaking them deepened her anguish.
It was true. She couldn't deny it. Ed, her best friend, the
man she had promised to marry, the man she had somehow
failed to protect, was gone.

"Oh, Carolyn." Helen stroked Carolyn's head, trying to
soothe her. "I'm so sorry."

She didn't understand. Carolyn brushed off Helen's
hand. "Leave me alone." When Helen's eyes widened in
surprise at Carolyn's curt tone, she continued, "Go away,
Helen. You can't help me. No one can."

But Helen was not so easily discouraged. No matter what
Carolyn said, she continued her attempts to comfort her.
Finally, Carolyn buried her head under the pillow and re-
fused to listen. Helen didn't understand that no one could
provide solace. Only a worthy person deserved solace, and
Carolyn was not worthy.

*   *   *

Dwight stared at the obviously distraught woman who had barged into one of the wards, demanding to speak to him. "If she won't listen to you," he said at last when he had heard her story, "I doubt I can help."

Helen Guthrie's brown eyes were filled with pain and her hands were clenched as if she were trying to control her emotions. "Please try, Doctor Hollins. You're my last hope."

He nodded, though there was no denying his reluctance. As a physician, he would have gone to anyone who was in the agony Helen described, and he would have tried to relieve the patient's suffering. But this was not an ordinary patient; it was Carolyn who needed help. A month ago, Dwight would have been confident that he could help her. Today, he feared that he would only worsen what appeared to be a very difficult situation. Still, he had to try, for he could not bear the thought of Carolyn's unhappiness.

Minutes later he rapped on the door to her room. "We need to talk."

"Go away." Her voice was so thick with tears that he barely recognized it. "I don't want to talk." This was what Helen had feared, that Carolyn would refuse to see him, just as she had refused Helen's attempts to comfort her.

"I'm not going away," Dwight said. Though Carolyn might be stubborn, so was he. "I'm prepared to stand here knocking on your door until you come out."

There was a long silence during which he feared that she would simply ignore him. Then Dwight heard the sound of footsteps, slow, almost shuffling, so different from Carolyn's normally light movements that he cringed. When the door opened, he hoped his expression did not betray his shock. He had known that Carolyn's face would be blotched from crying; he had expected that. What he had not expected was the dull, almost lifeless expression in her eyes. She looked like a person on the verge of death.

"Dwight, I know you mean well," Carolyn said, her

voice as flat and expressionless as her eyes. "You can't help me, though. No one can."

This was what Helen had told him, that Carolyn somehow felt that nothing and no one could provide comfort. It was not a rational thought, but in times of great stress, people were not always rational. Dwight had seen the way shock could affect a person.

"I thought the same thing once," he reminded her, "and you proved me wrong."

Carolyn shook her head. "This is different."

"Of course it is." A broken engagement could not compare to a fiancé's death. "What you're facing is much more serious. Still, a friend can help. I'm your friend, Carolyn, and I don't want you to be alone."

Though he had thought she might refuse, when he suggested that they go to the staff lounge, she agreed, albeit reluctantly. This was a positive sign, he told himself. She hadn't refused his offer completely. "It's all right to cry or even to scream if you want," Dwight said when they were in the former library. The fact that the room was empty was the second positive sign. "This war is horrible. It's cruel, and it's unfair." Dwight put his hand on top of Carolyn's. Hers was cold and—though he knew it was impossible—seemed to have shrunk. "Ed shouldn't have died." He was stating facts, hoping that somehow he could break through the wall she had built around her emotions. He wished he could somehow prod her into anger, for that would mean that the healing had begun. First shock, then anger. Dwight had seen the pattern and had experienced it himself.

Though he had thought she might continue to stare at the floor, Carolyn met his gaze. For the briefest of instants Dwight wished he hadn't seen the pain reflected in her eyes. No one should have to suffer that way.

"You don't understand," Carolyn said. "No one does."

"I may not understand everything you're feeling, but I know what it's like to deal with death."

She shook her head again. "You don't understand," she insisted. "You've never been in my situation."

"You're right," he agreed. "I did not lose my fiancée to death." Though his heart had ached when Louise rejected him, it hadn't taken long for Dwight to realize that it was his pride, not his heart, that had been bruised. Carolyn's situation was far more serious.

"It's not that." Carolyn turned her hand over and gripped his. "Oh, Dwight, I killed him. I killed Ed!"

Dwight was unable to mask his surprise. This, then, was the reason Carolyn was in such agony. Somehow, for some inexplicable reason, she believed she was culpable. It was up to him to convince her otherwise. "What do you mean? You couldn't have killed Ed."

Her grip tightened, and Dwight sensed that she was holding onto him as if he were a lifeline. This was good. In fact, it was very good. Perhaps speaking of her fears would be like lancing and cauterizing a wound. Perhaps it would be the first step toward healing.

Carolyn's eyes were clouded with pain as she said, "I may not have pulled the pin on the grenade, but I was responsible."

Dwight covered her hand with his other one, stroking it gently. "You're not making sense," he said as calmly as he could. "Why do you think you're responsible?"

Carolyn was silent for a long moment, her eyes searching his, asking a question that he could not identify. Did she think he would condemn her? No matter what she believed, he knew that she was innocent of Ed's death.

"Ed walked into danger deliberately. He wanted to be a hero. I knew that, and I tried to convince him to be sensible, but my letter didn't get to him in time. I failed him!"

Dwight wondered how many other women harbored this fear, that somehow they had contributed to their loved ones' deaths. "Carolyn, every man wants to be a hero, especially in the eyes of the woman he loves. I would venture to say that Ed wanted you to be proud of him, and that's why he volunteered. It wasn't a death wish. Ed had every reason to live." Dwight knew that if Carolyn loved him and had agreed to marry him, he would do everything humanly possible to ensure that he came back to her. Life with Carolyn would be the "happily ever after" that every man wanted. No one would willingly forfeit that.

"But what if . . . ?" Carolyn's voice was low, fervent, and so filled with pain that Dwight knew he would do anything in his power to ease that pain. "What if Ed knew I didn't love him?" When Dwight started to interrupt, Carolyn held up her free hand, stopping him. "What if," she asked, "Ed realized that I love you?"

Her words hit him with the force of a blow to the solar plexus, and for a second Dwight was unable to speak. Carolyn loved him! How many nights had he dreamed that he heard her speaking those words, only to wake, knowing that was one dream that would never come true? Carolyn's love had been a fantasy he had clung to in the dark hours after midnight when the future had seemed bleak. It had been a dream he had never dared to speak aloud, lest he somehow destroy his last chance at happiness. And yet, despite all odds, here was Carolyn, saying the words that would turn this cursed war from the worst to the best part of his life.

Dwight, the man who planned his future as if it were a military campaign, did one of the first impulsive acts of his adult life. Without stopping to think, he took both of Carolyn's hands in his and smiled at her. "I love you, too," he said. Her only reaction was a widening of her eyes as if in disbelief. Did she somehow think that he was saying this only to comfort her? She was wrong. He loved her, and he had wanted to tell her so for weeks.

Dwight slipped to the floor and knelt in front of Carolyn. "Sweetheart, this may not seem like the right time, but if there's one thing I've learned from this war, it's that each day is precious and that we shouldn't waste a single chance at happiness." She stared at him, almost as if he were speaking a foreign language. He had to make her understand. It was vital that she knew how he felt. Dwight took a deep breath, then blurted out, "I love you, Carolyn. Will you marry me?"

The remaining color drained from her face, but there was no hesitation as she said, "I can never marry you, Dwight. Never!"

Chapter Eleven

Carolyn frowned as she prepared for another day of work by slipping her feet into the rubber boots that had become a permanent part of her wardrobe since her transfer to the field hospital. She had wanted a change, and she had gotten exactly that. Though she and Helen had complained about the cramped conditions at the Goudot base hospital, they seemed palatial compared to the casualty clearing station. While the shortage of coal had meant that the Goudot mansion had been cold, at least it was dry. Here the staff dealt with rain and the inevitable mud as well as cold. They lived in tents. They ate in tents. They operated in tents. And those tents had no floors. As a result, the staff stood in ankle deep mud as they removed fragments of bones and shrapnel, trying to stanch bleeding and suture wounds. It was, Carolyn reflected as she hurried toward the large tent that served as the operating theater, a miracle that anyone survived the primitive conditions.

The only good thing she could say about life so close to the front was that she was almost too busy to grieve. Almost. The work was more physically demanding than in Goudot, the hours longer. By the time she returned to the tent that she shared with five other nurses, Carolyn was

150

always exhausted. By all rights, she should have slept well. And yet she did not. For her nights were disturbed by dreams that left her trembling, certain that nothing in this world would ever again be right, that the horrible emptiness that plagued her days would never disappear.

It should have been different. Though nursing was difficult, it was also rewarding. Carolyn and the doctors who fought death so valiantly were making a difference. One at a time, they were saving men's lives, and that was what was important. That was why she had come to France.

Carolyn slogged through the mud, trying not to think of the men they had not been able to save. It was normal, she knew, to have a higher mortality rate in the field hospitals than in base operations like Goudot. That it was understandable was no consolation, for Carolyn could not think in terms of mortality rates. These were men who should not have died. Though the politicians might claim that the cause was glorious, each time a soldier breathed his last, Carolyn thought of the loved ones whose lives would never be the same. Each time, she thought of Ed, and each time, she worried that Theo might be next.

Carolyn drew her coat tighter, wishing the rain would stop. Perhaps if the sun shone, her sorrow would lessen. Martha had told her that while her grief might never disappear, it would begin to subside. Her sister ought to know, for she had lost her husband in this horrible war. *Work helps*, Martha had written, when she had learned of Ed's death. That was the reason Martha herself had returned to teaching when her husband had died.

But work wasn't helping Carolyn. She felt as though all the sparkle had vanished from her life. She had lost not just Ed but also her sense of purpose. Though she tried to smile for the men, remembering how her humor had helped so many patients face surgery, Carolyn found that her jokes fell flat. She couldn't muster the energy to invent another of her grandmother's homilies, and she hadn't even laughed when she saw the clothespin that Helen had hidden between her uniforms when she unpacked her bag.

Ed wouldn't want you to grieve, Theo had written when the fighting had subsided and he had once again been able to write letters. Her brother was right. Unfortunately, knowing that did not stop Carolyn from mourning for the friend whose life had been cut short. She had reread Ed's letters so many times that she could quote whole passages. *All I want is for you to be happy*, he had told her. It was ironic, Carolyn reflected, that she and Ed had each sought the other's happiness, and they had both failed. Ed was gone. As for Carolyn, she wasn't happy, and she feared that she never again would be.

Carolyn opened the flap and entered the operating tent, trying not to gag at the stench of burned flesh and men's fears. If only the war would end! Then this horrible suffering would be over. Then she and the men could return home and rebuild their lives. It wouldn't be easy for any of them, but Carolyn was convinced they would succeed. Martha had done it; she could, too. Wordlessly, Carolyn took her place at the operating table, assisting one of the young doctors who, though skilled, did not seem as talented as Dwight.

Dwight. Carolyn cringed. He was another reason she wanted the war to end. Surely once she was back in Canela, she would be able to forget Dwight and the way he had looked when she refused his offer of marriage. She would be able to forget the sight of those hazel eyes darkened with pain and the frown that had crossed Dwight's face when she had repeated the word "never." At home she would be able to forget the longing and hopelessness she had seen in his expression the day she had left Goudot.

Carolyn handed the doctor a sponge. Though her hands moved mechanically, her thoughts continued to whirl, and despite her efforts, she could not prevent herself from thinking of Dwight and his unexpected proposal. At the time, she had not been certain who was more shocked by the impulsive gesture, herself or Dwight. She had stared at him, not quite believing her ears, but he had assured her that his question was not an act of chivalry, designed to heal her wounds. Dwight was serious. He wanted her to marry him. That was the problem. Carolyn couldn't marry Dwight. Not today, not ever. Marrying him would be the ultimate betrayal of Ed.

It was bad enough that she was afraid Ed had suspected how she felt about Dwight. Though Carolyn no longer believed that Ed had deliberately sought death, she was still plagued with guilt that she hadn't been able to love him the way he deserved to be loved. Ed had been a fine man, her neighbor and her best friend. He had deserved more than she had given him. Though she couldn't change what had happened, she wouldn't make mockery of her promises. She wouldn't marry anyone, especially not Dwight.

Carolyn stared at the patient before her. A faint smile crossed his face, as if whatever he dreamed under the anesthesia was pleasant. Unbidden, her thoughts turned to the memory of Dwight's face the day they had danced in the rain. He had been filled with both sorrow and skepticism when they began the dance. By the end he was smiling, a full-fledged grin, far different from the soldier's smile. Dwight had smiled at her, and then . . . Ruthlessly, Carolyn refused to remember how the dance had ended. There was no point in dwelling on something that should never have happened and which would never, ever be repeated.

As Carolyn helped the doctor bandage the patient's wound, Carolyn thought back to the days when she and Dwight had treated other men. Then she had felt satisfaction and even a sense of victory when they were able to save a severely wounded soldier. Now she felt nothing other than grief. That was another reason she could not consider marrying Dwight. Not only would it be a betrayal of Ed, but it would also be unfair to Dwight.

Dwight was a wonderful man. There was no denying that. But he was also a man who deserved a whole woman, not the empty shell Carolyn had become. They could never be together. They *would* never be together. If only she could stop dreaming of him!

If only he could stop dreaming of her! Dwight pulled a clean uniform out of the armoire and began to dress. There had been a time when he had whistled while he prepared for another day of surgery. There had been a time when even the rain had not been able to dampen his spirits. Now the days stretched in a monotonous chain. They were something to be endured, not anticipated. So much had changed, and it was his fault. He should have known better than to give into impulse. Look what his hasty words had caused: the loss of the best nurse he'd ever had. Though they tried, none of the other nurses was as competent as Carolyn. They waited for his orders rather than anticipating them, and while they tried to comfort the patients, their words fell short of Carolyn's little jokes that had proven so soothing.

Surgery had become an ordeal, a battle against death made all the more difficult by the absence of one of Dwight's most powerful weapons: Carolyn's laughter. Visiting the wards was almost as bad, for the patients seemed morose, and those who had known Carolyn asked when she would return, as if they realized that he was responsible for her leaving. The soldiers' mood only deepened Dwight's guilt. How could he have been so stupid? With just a few words, he had driven Carolyn away. He had heard that Miss Pierce had advised Carolyn not to accept the transfer to the field hospital, telling her she needed the continuity of a familiar setting to help her heal, but Carolyn had been adamant. The reason, Dwight knew, wasn't hard to find. He had given her a second shock at a time when she was already deeply wounded. No wonder she had fled. She wanted to distance herself from the source of pain.

Dwight buttoned his shirt and reached for his hairbrush. He hoped Carolyn was in less pain now, for he certainly was not. Though the days were awful, they paled compared to the nights. The double shifts he had been working should have guaranteed dreamless sleep. Instead the only thing that seemed to be guaranteed was that he would dream of Carolyn. Though the dreams varied, the aftermath did not. He would waken, filled with longing. He wanted to see her smile, to hear her laugh, and to hold her in his arms again.

Frowning, Dwight wielded the brush with more force than normal. This wasn't what he had planned. Dwight Hollins, the man who had developed a detailed schedule for his life, had never expected to fall in love with a woman like Carolyn. He had believed that the perfect wife for him would be a woman like Louise, a woman who would never invent a grandmother and who would never, ever wear a clothespin on her nose.

Carolyn was all wrong for him. He knew that. But he also knew that it was pointless to deny that the time he had spent with her made everything else in his life seem to pale in comparison. When he was with Carolyn, he felt alive. And now . . . Now he felt as if some vital part of him were missing.

He was a physician. As such, he knew the impossibility of hearts breaking or being lost. Those were poetic metaphors that he had scorned from the first time he had heard them. Dwight Hollins would never lose his heart. It would never break. Those were incontrovertible facts. What was also incontrovertible was the fact that he felt as if his heart had been wrenched from his body and that the only way he would once again be a whole man would be if Carolyn returned.

Grabbing his hat, Dwight strode across the courtyard toward the dining room. Though he had no appetite, he knew the folly of trying to operate without adequate nourishment. Still, he hated entering a room where he and Carolyn had once laughed together. Here, even more than in the operating theater, was where she had tried to convince him that laughter was an important part of life. He hadn't wanted to believe her. Laughter, he had thought, was frivolous, as unnecessary as an appendix. Now he realized the truth of Carolyn's words. She was right. Laughter was essential. And if he was going to have laughter in his life, he needed Carolyn.

Oh, how he needed her! He needed her in the operating room. He needed her in the wards. Most of all, he needed her in his arms. Dwight stopped in mid-stride. If he needed her, why was he letting her get away? He had made a mistake, asking her to marry him when she'd been overwhelmed with grief. Though he couldn't undo that, he could try again.

Carolyn had once accused him of being like a general, planning his life as if it were a military campaign. She had thought lack of spontaneity was a fault. Perhaps it wasn't, at least not for him. Dwight was good at planning; he was good at strategy. Where he failed was when he forgot that and acted without thinking. It was time to put his skills to work.

"Nurse Guthrie." When he had filled his tray with food that suddenly looked appetizing, Dwight took a seat next to Carolyn's former roommate. He tried not to notice how the other nurses quickly finished their breakfast, leaving Dwight and Helen alone at the table. Though he felt a twinge of regret that most of the nursing staff still seemed to regard him as an ogre, he could not regret the fact that he could now have a private conversation with Helen.

"What is it women want?" he asked. As he had crossed the courtyard, mentally planning his campaign, Dwight had realized that he was venturing into unknown and possibly hostile territory and would need assistance. Helen Guthrie, he reasoned, was uniquely positioned to give him that assistance. Not only had she been Carolyn's closest friend here, but she was also married. That meant that she had first-hand knowledge of love and courtship.

Helen gave him an appraising look. "Are you interested in women in general or one specific woman?"

There was no point in denying the obvious. "One woman. To put it bluntly, I need to know what Carolyn would like." He hated asking for help, but if he was going to succeed—and he would not admit the possibility of failure—he needed it.

The little smile that played at the corner of Helen's lips told Dwight she was enjoying his discomfiture. Helen was silent for a moment, making Dwight fear that she would refuse to answer. At last she spoke. "Carolyn never said it in so many words, but even though she was engaged, I suspect she was never wooed. Almost every woman would like a real courtship."

The eggs that had seemed delicious a second before lost their flavor. "A courtship like flowers, candy, and poetry?" This was worse than he'd feared. Dwight's sisters had had heated arguments over which element of courtship was the most important. Though he had dismissed their conversations, now he wished he had listened more carefully.

"Exactly." Helen smiled, and this time there was no doubt that she was laughing inwardly at his ignorance.

A courtship. Dwight blinked as he realized that it wasn't only Carolyn who had become engaged without one. Though he had placed a diamond on her left hand, he had never wooed Louise. In fact, he reflected, he hadn't actually asked her to marry him. He had simply bought the ring Louise had selected and given it to her on the day she had said she wanted to be engaged. Was that part of the reason Louise had eloped with the Ford repairman? Had Harold provided all the niceties that Dwight had not? Dwight clenched his jaw. He would not make the same mistake with Carolyn. If she wanted to be wooed, he would woo her. His step lighter than it had been in weeks, Dwight headed for the operating theater.

By late afternoon, his initial optimism had begun to fade. Helen had made it sound simple. Flowers, candy, poetry. Surely that couldn't be as difficult as repairing a torn artery. It was, Dwight could now attest, worse. Why had he picked winter in a war zone for his courtship? There were no flowers available in February; the supply of candy was meager; and the only poetry was written in French. Since his own command of the language was more meager than the supply of candy, he wasn't willing to give Carolyn poems. What if they weren't as romantic as the shopkeeper claimed? Though he had intended to buy all three things Helen claimed were needed for a proper wooing, Dwight returned from town with nothing more than a single tin of chocolates. This was not the most auspicious beginning.

Think like a general, he admonished himself. *Find another plan.* What was it his sisters had claimed was so romantic? Dwight wished there were time to ask them, even though it would mean that they would spend hours laughing at him. But time was one thing he did not have. He couldn't go on like this much longer. *Think!* Dwight closed his eyes, trying to recall the girls' whispered confidences. *He's so handsome. He said the most romantic things.* That was it. He would have to do his wooing in person.

Dwight frowned at the prospect. It was one thing to send a tin of candy. He didn't have to watch Carolyn's reaction when she received the package. He would never know if she had given the chocolates to other nurses or patients rather than eating them herself. But if he visited her, he was running the risk that she would refuse to see him. Dwight did not like risk. *Nothing ventured, nothing . . .* For the first time that day, Dwight grinned. He was starting to sound like Carolyn's fictitious grandmother. Surely that was a good sign.

* * *

She shouldn't be here. It was her half day off, and for once the sun was shining. She should take advantage of the pleasant weather to escape from the hospital, if only for a few minutes. Instead, she sat on the edge of her cot, too tired to even open a book. She had to shake this lethargy. It was interfering with everything, including her ability to assist the doctors. She knew what she needed to do. Finding the energy to do it was the problem.

"You have a visitor in the mess tent." One of Carolyn's tent mates stuck her head through the flap.

Carolyn looked up in surprise. She wasn't expecting anyone. Theo wasn't due for leave for another month, and though they were hoping to arrange some time together, they had both agreed that they wanted to meet away from the battle zone.

"Who is it, Margaret?" Even to Carolyn's ears, her voice sounded dull and lifeless. It was no wonder, when that was the way she felt.

The other woman shrugged. "He wouldn't tell me his name, but he's very handsome."

A tiny seed of hope lodged in Carolyn's heart. It couldn't be him, could it? And even if it was, she didn't want him here, did she? There was only one way to find out. "Thanks, Margaret." Carolyn grabbed her cape. As she headed toward the medium-sized tent that functioned as a general meeting place in addition to a dining room, a small shiver of anticipation went up her spine. The visitor could be someone else, perhaps one of Ed's friends. But it could also be . . .

He stood inside the tent. Though his clothing was mud-stained and his face lined with fatigue, Carolyn was certain she had never seen anything so wonderful in her life. The lethargy and sense of emptiness that had plagued her from the day she had arrived here were gone, replaced by a simple happiness. "Dwight!" Miss Pierce had been right when she had advised Carolyn to remain in the familiar surroundings of Goudot. It was surely only the sight of a familiar face that made Carolyn feel this way. She would have felt the same way if Helen had come. Of course she would.

Carolyn extended a hand in greeting. Though her heart pounded with excitement, she forced herself to speak slowly. "How did you get here?" she asked, when what she wanted to know was *why* he had come.

A crooked smile lit his face. "I commandeered a horse," he told her. By all rights, he should have released her hand. Common courtesy required only a brief touch. But Dwight seemed to have forgotten that, for he kept a firm grip on her. By all rights, she should have pulled her hand away. But Carolyn did not, for the warmth of Dwight's hand had started to dispel the cold that she had despaired would ever thaw.

"The horse wasn't as fast as an automobile." Dwight gave her another wry smile. "But at least I knew it wouldn't break down."

Though his words were commonplace, the way they made her feel was anything but common. For the first time since she had left Goudot, she felt as if she were once again a complete person.

"Why did you come?" The words escaped before she could stop them. She shouldn't ask. She shouldn't hope that he had come only to see her. Most likely, he was on his way to somewhere else. Perhaps he was delivering a message from Helen. That was it. Helen had wanted to come but couldn't because of her pregnancy.

Her legs suddenly weak, Carolyn sank onto a bench, pulling Dwight with her. He waited until she was facing him before spoke, and his eyes were warm with an emotion that Carolyn could not identify. "I missed you," he said.

The seed of hope that had appeared when Margaret told her she had a visitor sprouted leaves. "Aren't the other nurses capable?" Carolyn wouldn't let herself believe that there was anything personal in this visit.

Dwight turned her hand over and began to trace the lines on her palm. It was the lightest of touches, and yet the sensations his fingertips created were anything but casual. Shivers of delight raced from Carolyn's hand up her arm.

"The others aren't as good as you." Dwight raised his eyes and waited until she met his gaze. "That's not why I came," he said. "I won't try to convince you to return to Goudot because I need you as a nurse. The fact is, I miss *you*, Carolyn, not your nursing."

Blood rushed to Carolyn's face. He missed her. Dwight missed her. And, oh, how wonderful that felt! Though several men in Canela had vowed eternal love, no one had said words that touched Carolyn's heart the way Dwight's simple declaration did. Even when he had called her "darling," Ed had not . . .

Ed! Carolyn bit the inside of her cheek. What was she doing, harboring fantasies that could never come true? What kind of woman was she?

"I won't change my mind," she said, tugging her hand free from Dwight's. "I won't go back, and I won't marry you."

If her words and her gesture bothered him, Dwight gave no sign. "Did I ask you to?" He gestured toward the saddlebags that lay on a table next to him. "I brought a Thermos of tea and some of those pastries that you like. I was hoping you'd share them with me."

It was a simple request. There was no reason she should refuse. After all, refusing would not bring Ed back; it would merely be rude. And if she accepted, Carolyn would have another memory to help her through the lonely future.

"Thank you. I'd like that."

It was too cold to sit outside, so they spent the afternoon inside the mess tent, drinking tea, eating pastries, talking of everything and nothing. Carolyn recounted her experiences as a casualty clearing nurse; Dwight reported the progress of the patients she had known in Goudot. They spoke of the weather and the war, of food and fears. The one topic they never touched was Dwight's proposal of marriage.

Carolyn was happy that he did not repeat his proposal. Of course she was, for they both knew what her response must be. And yet as the afternoon waned, she couldn't help wondering why he said nothing. Could it be that he regretted his impulsive action? Dwight, after all, was not given to impulse. Perhaps he was relieved that she had refused. But if that was true, why had he come, and why had he told her he missed her?

Dwight glanced at his watch and frowned. "I'm not sure how often I can get away," he said as he rose to his feet and reached for the saddlebags. He looked down at Carolyn, his expression earnest. "Would I be welcome if I came again?"

It would be wrong. He would be wasting his time. Carolyn knew that. But as she opened her mouth to forbid him to return, she heard herself say, "I'd like that."

And that night, for the first time since she had learned of Ed's death, Carolyn's sleep was undisturbed by nightmares.

Chapter Twelve

"He's courting you," Margaret said as she coiled her hair into a bun.

"That's ridiculous." Both the idea of a courtship and the blush that stained Carolyn's cheeks were ridiculous. Thank goodness the other nurses had left, and only she and Margaret remained in the tent. This was a conversation Carolyn did not want overheard, particularly since she was unable to keep that telltale color from stealing onto her face. Carolyn knew there was speculation about her and Dwight, created by his visits and the letters that arrived almost every day. Her reaction to Margaret's declaration would only add fuel to the fire.

"Dwight's a friend. That's all. He knows I'm lonely; that's why he comes here."

Margaret raised an eyebrow as she skewered her bun. "Then why do none of the other nurses have 'friends' "— she gave the word an ironic twist—"who send them books and candy?"

Carolyn had no answer. The truth was, she had been surprised when the beautiful leather-bound book of poetry had arrived. To her knowledge, there was no place in Goudot that sold English language books. When she had asked

163

Dwight, he had told her that he had asked Helen to buy a copy in England. Her pregnancy now obvious, Helen had been forced to return home. Carolyn had known that. What she hadn't known was that Dwight corresponded with Helen and appeared to have enlisted her aid.

"And why," Margaret continued, "does no one else have a suitor who somehow manages to find time to visit, even though he's obviously overworked and exhausted like the rest of us?"

"Perhaps he wants a change of scenery." Carolyn was grasping at straws; she knew that, but she also knew that she wasn't going to give Margaret the satisfaction of admitting that she had asked herself the same questions.

Margaret's hoot told Carolyn that she found her explanation incredible. "Are you trying to convince me that the good doctor comes here—mere miles from the front—because he wants a change of scenery? Carolyn, the man isn't crazy. He's in love."

Carolyn wasn't sure of that. After all, though his behavior was suspiciously similar to the traditional courtship rituals, since that afternoon in Goudot, Dwight had never once mentioned love or marriage. He had acted as if he had expected her refusal to return to Goudot and as if her refusal to marry him was of no significance. That was good. Of course it was.

"It's not love," she told Margaret. "It's friendship."

Margaret raised her hands in a gesture of surrender. "I give up! If you want to delude yourself, go ahead. I know the truth, and I'm quite certain you do, too."

Self-delusion. Helen had accused her of that months ago, telling Carolyn that she and Dwight were in love but were trying to deny it. The truth was, Carolyn no longer tried to deny it. She loved Dwight with all her heart. But that didn't change the fact that she could not consider marrying him. Other women married after their husbands or fiancés died. Carolyn knew that and approved of it. In fact, she hoped her sister Martha would one day remarry. But other women's situations were different. Those women were not living with the knowledge that they had failed their men. Carolyn could not undo the mistakes she had made, but she would not repeat them.

"Do you know what today is?" Dwight asked. It was two days later, and he'd arrived in time to spend part of her half-day off with her. As he had on his last visits, he appeared visibly tired, his face lined with exhaustion, yet his eyes sparkled as if he looked forward to their time together as much as she did.

"Am I to assume that today is something special?" This year for the first time, she had forgotten Valentine's Day until one of Dwight's letters had mentioned it. What had she forgotten this time?

"Indeed, it is special." Dwight led her to the table where they spent rainy days, then sat on the bench, turning so that he was facing her. "Today is the first day of spring," he said and reached for her hands. "If you've read Tennyson, you know what that means: a young man's fancy turns to love."

Though Carolyn hadn't read Tennyson, she had heard the phrase, for Emily had accused Theo of falling into love each spring and falling out of love three months later, as if the changing seasons regulated his feelings. When they had spoken of Theo, she and Emily had laughed. Carolyn wasn't laughing now. This was probably the least romantic spot on earth: a mess tent that smelled of stale food and mud, a place where instead of soft, lyrical music, the silences were punctuated by the sound of distant artillery fire. And yet, Carolyn could not ignore the fire that she saw in Dwight's eyes or the earnestness she heard in his voice. In another time and place, in another life, her heart would have sung with happiness that this wonderful man was sitting there, looking at her as if she were the most precious being on earth. Instead, her heart began to pound with fear that he would utter the words that would destroy their friendship.

Dwight raised her hands to his lips and pressed a soft kiss on them. "I love you, Carolyn." The gesture was sweetly romantic and the words the ones every woman longed to hear. They should have kindled a warmth deep inside her. Instead, Carolyn felt as if someone were tightening a band around her heart. Dwight smiled at Carolyn, apparently not sensing her inner turmoil. "Please say you'll marry me."

Carolyn closed her eyes as she tried to fight the pain that threatened to engulf her. "Oh, Dwight!" She blinked, hoping to hold back her tears. "I can't."

His eyes darkened, and she saw confusion on his face. "I don't understand. Was I wrong in thinking you loved me?"

A coward would lie, but Carolyn was not a coward. "You weren't mistaken. I do love you." It was the first time she had spoken the words aloud since the day she had learned of Ed's death. It was odd, how right it felt to admit her love when she knew that it was wrong to love Dwight. Worse yet was the hope that the simple phrase lit in Dwight's eyes. Perhaps she should have lied; perhaps that would have been kinder.

"Then why won't you marry me?"

Carolyn stared at the tent wall, wishing there were a way to make this easier. "Because I can't." And, oh, how she wished that weren't true! It wasn't hard to conjure the image of herself married to Dwight. She could picture them in a country home, with big old trees in the front yard, one of them holding a swing where their children played. She could picture herself cooking dinner for Dwight, then waiting until he returned from a late house call to share it with him. But those were fantasies that would never come true.

Though she tried to tug her hands away, Dwight kept them clasped in his. His hands were warm and comforting, and that made Carolyn feel worse. Why was it that she kept hurting the men she loved?

"If you think it's too soon," Dwight said, "I can wait. I understand if you want a full year's mourning." That had been the traditional period before the war, but now couples, apparently sharing Dwight's belief that not a single day should be wasted, often married more quickly. That might be right for them, but it was wrong for Carolyn.

"I can't marry you, Dwight. Not now; not a year from now." Though Carolyn hated the pain that her words caused, she couldn't let him continue to hope, not when she knew that her answer would never change.

"Why?" It was only one word, yet it sounded as if it were wrenched from deep inside Dwight.

"It would be wrong."

He gave her a long appraising look. "Because of Ed?"

Carolyn nodded.

"But he's gone."

"I know." That was the problem. If the war had ended and Ed were still alive, perhaps there could be another answer. As it was, there was no hope.

Carolyn frowned as she pulled out a piece of stationery and prepared to answer a fortnight's worth of correspondence. Though she normally replied the next day, for the past two weeks she had been unable to do more than scan the letters, wishing for an hour's respite. The days since Dwight's last visit had been tumultuous ones, for March 21 had marked more than the start of spring. It was also the beginning of the enemy's latest offensive, what some were calling the Emperor Battle. The combination of poisonous gas and the greatest artillery barrage of the war meant that every field hospital on the Western Front was flooded with wounded men. Though the staff worked around the clock, there were times when it felt as if they were making no progress, as if two wounded arrived for every one they treated.

Today was the first day that they had been able to tend to every injured soldier, and Carolyn had returned to her sleeping tent an hour earlier than usual. Though she was exhausted, she did not want to delay her correspondence any longer. Carolyn slid her brother's letter from the envelope, then closed her eyes, remembering how often she had answered first Ed's, then Theo's epistles. And now. Now she went whole days without thinking of Ed, and when she did, it was becoming more and more difficult to remember what he looked like. It seemed as if Ed were fading from her memory the way the daguerreotypes from the War Between the States had faded with age. Carolyn hated that. Somehow it felt like the ultimate betrayal, worse even than her feelings for Dwight.

Carolyn frowned again. She didn't have to close her eyes to picture Dwight. He was always there, hovering at the edges of her mind. When she assisted a doctor in the operating tent, she remembered Dwight's skill. When the mailman handed her a letter, she remembered Dwight waiting for an envelope from Louise. And when it rained, she remembered how she and Dwight had danced together. Thoughts of Dwight were crisp and fresh, while memories of Ed were blurred and faded. That was so very, very wrong!

Resolutely, Carolyn re-read Theo's letter. *What's wrong, Sis? I'm worried, because your letters don't sound like you.* Carolyn clenched her pen. Could she do nothing right? The last thing she wanted was to add to Theo's worries. He had enough of those, being so close to the front, never knowing when the next offensive would put him in the midst of constant shelling. Fortunately, Theo's premonitions earlier this year had proven unfounded, and he was still safe. That was the one blessing 1918 had brought.

Carolyn scribbled a quick note to her brother, trying to

make him smile with images of his fastidious sister standing ankle-deep in mud, wearing one of the least flattering aprons mankind had invented over a dull gray uniform. *You may have vowed never to eat another canned tomato once the war ends*, she wrote. *I made a different vow. I can promise you that I will never, ever own another gray garment.*

When she had sealed her letter to Theo, Carolyn opened one from Martha. *I know it may seem impossible*, her sister had written, *but try to find something good each day, some reason you're glad to be alive. That's how I dealt with Henry's death.* Carolyn bit the end of her pen. What was good about her life? Unbidden, the image of Dwight opening his saddlebags and pulling out a Thermos leaped into Carolyn's mind. She shook her head, trying to dismiss the thought. It was foolish and frivolous to think of Dwight's visits. What was important was the work she was doing and the lives she was helping to save. Martha was right. Carolyn needed to focus on what was important. She could do that. She would think of nothing other than nursing. She would be as single-minded as Dwight.

With a cry of disgust, Carolyn tossed her pen onto the table. Why did everything remind her of Dwight?

If only everything didn't remind him of her! Dwight stared at the nurse who stood on the opposite side of the operating table. "Scalpel," he repeated. The woman reached for the instrument, nearly dropping it in her hurry to hand it to him. Carolyn would not have fumbled. Even her first day assisting him, she had shown more skill than this nurse, who had years of experience.

"You can prepare the next patient," he said as he tied the final suture on Private Canfield's leg.

The nurse turned to the man in the next bed and began to explain what would happen. Though her voice was low and soothing, Dwight saw that the man remained anxious, his eyes darting nervously from the nurse to Dwight. That hadn't happened when Carolyn joked with the patients. Carolyn had been so good at reassuring them that the men frequently regarded Dwight as ancillary to his nurse rather than the other way around.

Dwight frowned. This was ridiculous! He had work to do, and he couldn't do it unless he stopped thinking of Carolyn. He had to stop thinking of her, but Dwight knew the only way that would happen would be if Carolyn agreed to marry him and return here. That didn't appear likely.

Dwight had been surprised by Carolyn's second refusal and had wanted to ask Helen Guthrie's opinion. He hadn't, though, for there were some things a man didn't like to put in writing, and rejection was one of them. He had tried to understand Carolyn's reaction. Perhaps it was only that his timing had been off. That must be it. Carolyn needed to mourn Ed a bit longer. Then she would agree to marry Dwight. Of course she would. Hadn't she said that she loved him?

"Is something wrong, Doctor?"

Dwight blinked at the nurse's question. Had she somehow read his thoughts? Shocked, he realized that he had been staring into space, so lost in his reverie that he had forgotten his work. No wonder the nurse was regarding him with concern.

"No!" Dwight replied with more emphasis than normal. No, nothing was wrong, and no, he wouldn't continue acting like a lovesick youth. He would get his life back on kilter, and there was only one way to do that. As soon as the shift was completed, he would put his plan into motion.

"Why don't you just ask for a transfer?" The other physician's expression was sympathetic when he agreed to cover for Dwight. "Wouldn't it be easier to court her if you were together?"

Dwight shrugged. "Nothing in my life has been easy. Why should this be any different?" Besides, if this trip ended the way he hoped it would, he and Carolyn would soon be together—here in Goudot.

By all rights he should have been exhausted by the time he reached the field hospital. He had slept only a few hours the night before, and it had been weeks since he had had the luxury of a full night's sleep. But, though weariness had settled in his bones, Dwight could not suppress the excitement that surged through his veins as he tied the horse to a post. Soon! Soon he would see her, and then maybe . . .

Her face looked thinner than before, the lines between her eyes deeper, as if she too had had little sleep. Her skirt was wrinkled and spattered with mud, a fact Dwight noted when she gave it an apologetic glance. As if he cared! It mattered not a whit whether she wore nurse's gray or that beautiful red silk dress she had donned on Christmas Day. He smiled when his eyes caught a sparkle on her bodice and he realized that she was wearing the brooch he had given her. Surely that was a good sign. The rain that continued to fall certainly wasn't a favorable omen. Unless . . .

"You look like you need some cheering," he told Carolyn when he had greeted her.

The swift smile that had lit her face when she'd first seen him faded. "The new enemy offensive means that we have more wounded than ever before. Oh, Dwight, I feel so helpless when we lose one."

How well he knew the feeling! "I know," he said softly, taking her hand in his again. "The only thing that helps is thinking of the ones you manage to save."

"But I wish . . ."

"I know." Carolyn needed cheering, and maybe if he could raise her spirits, she would give him the answer he wanted. Dwight gave her hand a little squeeze. "A wise woman once told me that laughter heals, and so does dancing in the rain." He gestured toward the tent flap. "I'm not

very good at telling jokes, but it's raining, and I still remember the steps to the Castle Gavotte."

Her attempt to smile wrenched his heart. Never before,
not even the day she had learned of Ed's death, had he seen
such hopelessness on her face. "Oh, Dwight, I know what
you're trying to do," Carolyn said, her voice filled with
sadness. "It won't work. I feel like I'll never be happy
again."

He knew that feeling, too. But he also knew how to cure
it. Whether she recognized it or not, Carolyn needed him,
just as he needed her. It was up to him to make her understand that together they could find happiness. "I could
help, if you'd let me."

The furrows between her eyes deepened. "What do you
mean?"

He wouldn't take her to the table where she had refused
him the last time. Instead, he led her toward the tent's sole
window. Perhaps the sight of the rain would remind her of
those magic moments they had spent in each other's arms.

"You know I love you, Carolyn," he said slowly, willing
her to listen, willing her to give them both a chance at
happiness. "If you marry me, I'll spend the rest of my life
making you happy." When she started to speak, he shook
his head, needing to finish his declaration. So much hung
in the balance: her happiness, his, their future. Surely she
would see that marriage was the answer. "I may not always
succeed the first time, but I'll keep trying until I do make
you happy."

Carolyn was silent for a long moment, and he could see
the indecision on her face. Surely that was a good sign. In
the past, she had refused immediately. Today she hadn't.
That must mean that she was considering his proposal. But
then she spoke.

"I can't."

Dwight clenched his teeth. "Can't or won't?" He understood that she felt loyalty to Ed. Carolyn wouldn't be the

woman he loved if she didn't. But loyalty was one thing. Throwing away happiness was another.

"Is there a difference?"

"I think so. I've told you I'll wait until you're ready. Believe me, Carolyn. I've thought about this." Dwight frowned, remembering how often he had thought about her refusal. "I can see no reason why you *can't* marry me."

Carolyn stared at him for a long moment, those blue eyes that he had once thought as deep as the summer sky now filled with pain. "Then I guess the answer is that I won't." Her voice was firm, leaving him no glimmer of hope. It was not the answer he wanted. Even worse, there was a finality in her tone that said she would never change her mind.

"How can you do this?" he demanded, trying to push back the pain of Carolyn's rejection. This was worse—so much worse—than Louise's elopement. Louise had hurt his pride; Carolyn was breaking his heart. "How can you throw away our chance at happiness?" Carolyn was the only woman he would ever love. Dwight knew that if she refused to marry him, he would spend the rest of his life alone.

"Happiness needs a firm foundation," she said, her lips quivering and her eyes filling with tears. "We don't have one."

Dwight shook his head. She was wrong. He had to convince her of that, for everything worthwhile depended on her. "You're mistaken, Carolyn. Love is our foundation, and it's stronger than anything on earth."

Her mouth tightened, and she thrust her chin forward defiantly, though tears threatened to tumble down her cheeks. "The answer is still no."

She wasn't going to listen. No matter what he said, no matter what he did, she was going to destroy their chance at happiness because of some misguided sense of loyalty.

"All right." Dwight knew when he was defeated. Anger,

frustration, and a pain worse than any he had ever experienced welled up inside him. He looked at the woman he loved and shook his head slowly. "I've asked you to marry me three times. I won't do it again."

Dwight reached for his saddlebag, unable to bear the thought of everything Carolyn was throwing away. When he reached the tent flap, he turned and faced Carolyn one last time. "If you ever come to your senses and realize that you love me enough to take a chance on happiness, you know where I am. But next time you'll be the one who holds out her heart and risks having it stomped on. I won't do that again."

Chapter Thirteen

She ought to be happy. Carolyn unpinned her cap and laid it on the small chest that served as both a nightstand and a dressing table. Though no one was certain why General Ludendorff had stopped the western offensive that had begun on the first day of spring, there were no complaints. The respite, even if it was a temporary one, was the answer to many prayers.

Carolyn bent at the waist and began to brush her hair. Like the rest of the staff, she was thankful for the lull in the shelling which meant that there were no men waiting in the cold rain for triage. Carolyn was equally thankful that Theo was safe. As the battle had raged, she had checked the map someone had pinned to a mess tent wall and had been relieved to see that her brother's company was further north, away from the worst of the recent fighting. Though Carolyn knew that no trench was completely safe, the fact that Theo had not been in combat helped to allay her fears.

She winced as the brush tangled in her hair. Though lessened, nothing could stop her from worrying, for Theo had written again of his premonitions. This time he told her he was having nightly dreams of being in the midst of great, unending darkness. *There's no pain*, he wrote, *just a void darker than the blackest night.* When she had read his words, Carolyn's heart had begun to thud with dread, and it had taken every ounce of strength she could muster to remind herself that Theo's last fears had been unfounded. This, she told herself, would be another false alarm. Her brother was safe and away from the fighting. She should be, if not happy, at least content.

Carolyn finished brushing her hair, then began to gather her laundry. The sun was finally shining. That and the thought of dry, clean stockings would surely be enough to lighten her spirits. Yesterday she had received a long, newsy letter from Helen, in which her friend insisted that she was bored being home and that the thrill of knitting booties quickly faded. As she had turned the pages and read of Helen's newfound domesticity, Carolyn had smiled.

Her life was on an even keel, as good as it could be until the war ended. Carolyn ought to be happy, and yet she was not. The reality was, she was unhappier than she had ever been. The first sharp pain of Ed's death had faded, replaced by a constant ache that sapped her energy and left her feeling drained, no matter what she did. Martha would say that this was the normal progression of grieving. But it was not normal, for the ache that refused to disappear had nothing to do with Ed. This pain and the accompanying lassitude were all because of Dwight.

It was absurd! Carolyn bundled her soiled aprons into a laundry bag, giving the pouch an extra punch. She had done the right thing when she had refused Dwight's proposal. Of course she had. She couldn't marry Dwight; she couldn't even consider it. Carolyn frowned as she looked at her uniforms, trying to decide which needed to be laundered. Perhaps she should have been one of those Indian women she had read about who climbed onto their husbands' funeral pyres. Perhaps that would have been easier than living with the guilt and the sense that she had failed

Ed. Carolyn didn't know. All she knew was that she couldn't continue this way. She couldn't continue to dream of Dwight each night and to find herself spending the days looking outside, hoping for a glimpse of him approaching on his horse. He wouldn't be back; there was no question about that. So why did she keep looking for him?

"Why are you inside?" Margaret demanded as she opened the tent flap. "The sun is out, and we have no new patients. This is so close to a miracle that I want to believe it's the end of the war."

Carolyn chose not to respond to Margaret's question. Instead, she nodded slowly as she considered her tent mate's final sentence. "How I wish that were true! I want to go home." Carolyn had never been homesick, not in the usual sense. This longing to be back in Canela was different. Even more than the people and the familiar places, she missed the simplicity and, yes, the innocence, of life before the war. Though her mind knew that she could not go back in time, Carolyn's heart refused to believe it.

"It won't be the same, you know."

Carolyn blinked in surprise. She knew she hadn't voiced her thoughts. How had Margaret sensed them? "My sisters and brother and I will be together again," she countered. At home the bluebonnets would bloom; Spanish moss would drape the tree branches; life would continue as it had for generations.

Margaret's blue eyes filled with sympathy as she shook her head. "You'll all be different than you remember. The war has changed everyone. And . . ." Her face darkened, and she swallowed deeply before she finished her sentence. "Not everyone will be going home."

Carolyn looked at her hands and the ring that she still wore. Perhaps it was foolish, but she had been unable to remove Ed's ring. The gold band with its modest diamond was all that remained of him other than Carolyn's memories. Though she did her best to keep them alive, the memories continued to fade a bit each day. Carolyn feared that if she no longer wore his ring, Ed would disappear completely. She couldn't let that happen.

"At least the killing would be over," she said quietly. And maybe if she were home, she would be able to build a new life, one that held no dreams of handsome doctors and country homes where hazel-eyed children played on an old swing.

Margaret was silent for a moment. Then she flashed Carolyn an impish grin. "What do you miss the most?"

Carolyn recognized the ploy for what it was, an attempt to raise her spirits. Though she doubted this or anything else would have permanent effects, she was willing to play the game. Anything was better than thoughts of dreams that would never come true.

What did she miss most besides a normal life? "Being able to fill the bathtub with hot water and sit in it for an hour. Maybe that would soak off all this mud." Carolyn wrinkled her nose as she looked at her mud-caked stockings. Though the nurses had complained about the limited laundry and bathing facilities in Goudot, in comparison to the conditions here, the base hospital at Goudot was a first class hotel.

When Margaret laughed, Carolyn countered with a question of her own. "What about you? What do you miss most?"

Margaret's reply came quickly. "Dancing." She smiled, obviously remembering her life before the war. "I loved those dances that Vernon and Irene Castle invented." With a quick pirouette, Margaret began the Castle Gavotte. "Did you ever learn this one?"

"Yes." Carolyn closed her eyes, trying to block the pain. Margaret's question was innocent. She had no way of knowing that dancing was yet another thing Carolyn did not want to remember, for it reminded her of Dwight. Sadly, everything reminded her of Dwight.

* * *

"What's wrong?" Art Webster demanded.

Dwight turned a startled look at the man who sat across from him in the staff lounge. Art was the only physician who had been in Goudot longer than Dwight, and while the two men were not close, they kept the same hours and frequently ate breakfast together. This morning, though the dining room was relatively crowded, they had been the only people at a table for eight. They had eaten in silence. If Art had wanted to speak to him, why hadn't he done it then, not now when anyone could see that Dwight was reading and would not welcome an interruption?

"Nothing's wrong," Dwight replied. *Nothing that he intended to discuss with Art.* He had no intention of telling Art that coming here was a bit like probing an open sore, for each time he entered the room, he remembered the times he and Carolyn had been here together. "Why do you ask?"

"Let me think." The sarcasm that tinged the other doctor's voice was as unexpected as his question. "It could be that every nurse who's assigned to you cringes in fear of your wrath."

"That's not true." What was true was that the newly arrived nurses seemed to lack the common sense that God gave a grasshopper. If Dwight was sharp with his demands, it was merely because that seemed to be the only way to get the nurses' attention.

"Isn't it?" Art's lips curved in a mocking smile. "If that's not the reason, perhaps it's because the patients say you're so distracted when you examine them they're afraid you'll miss something critical. One man said you wouldn't notice if his good leg fell off."

"That's not true!" Dwight was a good doctor, an excellent doctor, in fact. Just because he had once—only once, mind you—begun to examine the wrong leg didn't mean that he was preoccupied.

Art shook his head, as if in sympathy. "If you don't believe those reasons, shall we consider the fact that the book you're reading is upside down?"

"It is not!" Dwight looked down at the book that he'd been holding for the past half hour. To his chagrin, though his finger marked a passage, he could not read it, for the book was, as Art had pointed out, upside down. "Oh."

"Look, Dwight." This time there was no sarcasm in the other doctor's voice. "I don't claim to know you well. No one here does. But it appears to me that you're pining for that spunky nurse."

Dwight started to deny the allegation, then realized the futility of it. "If your diagnosis were correct," he said. "Not, of course, that I think it is. But if by some possibility it were correct, what would you prescribe?"

Art's lips started to curve upward; then as Dwight frowned, he bit back his smile. "Don't let her get away. You'd be a fool if you did."

He was not a fool! Though Dwight had heard many epithets, no one had called him a fool. Bridling at the allegation, he took a deep breath before he responded. "It's not that easy. What I want doesn't matter. What's important is how Carolyn feels." And Carolyn had left Dwight no doubt at all of her feelings.

Art leaned forward, his expression earnest. "She's bonnet over boots in love with you," he said. "That was plain to all of us." Art gave Dwight a wry smile. "I don't mind telling you that the rest of us were more than a little envious of the looks she used to give you."

Dwight remembered those looks. They had warmed his days and fueled his dreams. Unfortunately, now all they did was frustrate him, for they were part of the past. Carolyn had made it clear that there would be no future. "Looks don't matter," he said. "Actions do. And Carolyn's have said that she doesn't want me."

Art shook his head. "I don't believe that."

"I do." That was the problem.

"Suture."

Carolyn handed it to the doctor, trying not to remember the times she had worked with Dwight. Then there had been little need for spoken commands. She had known what he would require and had taken pride in being able to help him. She was helping here. There was no denying that, just as there was no denying that it wasn't the same.

Nothing was the same. The fighting had resumed, and though the battle itself was miles away near Ypres, the less badly wounded men were brought here because the closest field hospitals were overflowing with patients. Carolyn tried not to cringe at the thought of how many men must be involved in this new offensive if they were sending wounded so far from the battle lines. The brief hope they had all cherished that the war might be ending when General Ludendorff had withdrawn in early April had been dashed by the realization that the enemy was intensifying its efforts. It was obvious they wanted to defeat the French and English now, before America could send in enough troops to turn the tide of war.

"Forceps."

Mechanically, Carolyn assisted the doctor. She wouldn't think about anything other than the tasks at hand. She wouldn't think of Dwight, and she most certainly wouldn't think of the future that stretched so bleakly before her.

By the time her shift was over, Carolyn's feet and back ached, and the pain that radiated through her cheeks told her she had been clenching her teeth. Would this war ever end? There were times when she doubted it would.

"Carolyn."

Carolyn looked up, surprised to see Margaret standing near the operating tent, a large umbrella opened over her. Why was she here? Though Helen had occasionally waited for Carolyn when she had wanted to persuade Carolyn to go to town or if she had needed a sympathetic ear, Margaret had never done that. Quickly, Carolyn ducked under the umbrella and stared at her tent mate, trying to guess why she was here.

"What's wrong?" Carolyn demanded when she saw the lines of sorrow etched on Margaret's face. A shiver ran down Carolyn's spine, and she said a silent prayer that she was misreading her friend's expression. Maybe the reason Margaret had waited for Carolyn wasn't personal. Maybe nothing was wrong. Maybe Margaret wanted to ask Carolyn for a favor.

Margaret shook her head, refusing to answer as she led the way into the mess tent. "Sit down," she said, and her voice cracked with emotion. Carolyn's dread grew. She had been deluding herself. Something was terribly wrong, and that something was directly related to Carolyn. That was the only reason for Margaret's behavior.

"What is it?" Carolyn demanded. "Tell me."

Margaret slid an arm around Carolyn's shoulders. If she hadn't already been worried, the gesture would have frightened Carolyn, for Margaret was not a woman given to physical contact. "It's your brother," Margaret said gently.

Theo? Carolyn felt the world begin to darken. "What about Theo?" Somehow she managed to force the words through lips that felt frozen with fear.

Margaret squeezed her shoulder. "Theo's battalion was attacked." Her eyes brimmed with unshed tears as she looked at Carolyn. "There's no easy way to say this, Carolyn. Everyone is presumed dead."

Everyone dead. Theo dead. The words whirled inside Carolyn's head like fallen leaves before a storm. She heard them repeat and repeat, but they made no sense. They were words, nothing more. They had no connection to her. They couldn't. This was a nightmare. Any minute now she would awaken back home in Canela.

"No!" Carolyn closed her eyes and shook her head violently. "I won't believe it! There's some mistake." But even as she spoke, Carolyn knew there was no mistake. This was not a nightmare. No matter how she wanted to believe that she was dreaming, she was not. This was real.

Margaret began to stroke Carolyn's back, trying to comfort her the way a parent would a small child. "I wish there were something I could say to make this easier."

But there was nothing. Carolyn struggled to her feet, filled with pain and anguish and the knowledge that nothing would ever be the same again. "He knew this was coming," she said as tears began to roll down her cheeks. "He told me he had dreamed of endless darkness. This is what he meant. Oh, Theo!" Carolyn wrapped her arms around her waist as sobs wracked her frame. "Theo! Oh, Theo!" she repeated.

The rain poured on the roof; in the distance artillery boomed; but neither reverberated in her mind the way Margaret's words did. Everyone dead. Carolyn closed her eyes, trying to block out the image of her brother lying still on some blood-stained battlefield. In its place, she pictured Theo and Emily running through their yard in Canela, playing tag. The image changed like the design in a kaleidoscope, and she saw him teaching Emily to hit a baseball, while Carolyn and Martha sat on the sidelines, cheering. Another shift of the pattern and there was Emily, bent over the engine of a Model T with Theo standing next to her, teaching her the mysteries of Henry Ford's creation.

Carolyn forced her eyes open and stared out the window. It was another rainy day in France, no different from a hundred others. But for Carolyn and all the others who had lost loved ones, today was unlike any other day. She clenched her fists as the memories washed over her. It was impossible to remember a time when Theo had not been part of her life. Now that time was over. He would never again run or laugh. He would never again play ball or fix an automobile. He would never again do anything.

"How can I help?"

Carolyn dashed the tears from her eyes. "You can't," she said. There was nothing anyone could do or say. "I need to be alone."

And so, although it was pouring rain, Carolyn buttoned her coat and went outside. Her feet moved mechanically, her eyes barely registering her surroundings as she walked down the narrow tree-lined road that led away from the battle zone. In another month, the poplars would be covered with leaves; today they looked as dead as . . . *No!* she cried. Her brother wasn't dead. It couldn't be true. But it was. The emptiness in her heart told her that.

Carolyn walked and walked, ignoring the pain in her calves. That was nothing compared to the pain inside her heart. She would welcome physical pain if it meant that this horrible emptiness deep inside her would end.

Mud, thick and viscous, squished beneath her boots, and she started to slip. How ironic, Carolyn thought as she stretched out her arms to regain her balance. Her world, which a year ago had seemed so stable, was gone. The sunshine and happiness had been replaced by rain and a sorrow too deep for words. Nothing was the same. Nothing would ever be the same again.

Carolyn took another careful step. Somehow it seemed terribly important to keep walking, as if the simple act of putting one foot in front of another would restore order to her life. It wouldn't, of course. Both Theo and Ed were gone, and nothing would bring them back. Carolyn had believed that by coming to France, she could help keep them safe. How wrong she had been! This horrible, horrible war was taking everyone she loved. First Ed, then Theo. Next Dwight.

As the thought hit her with the force of a blow, Carolyn grasped a tree trunk to keep from falling. It couldn't happen. Could it? Could Dwight be the next? Though Goudot had been lucky, Carolyn knew that the enemy frequently shelled hospitals. Was Dwight even now in mortal danger? She swallowed, trying to dislodge the lump in her throat that was making it so difficult to breathe. She couldn't lose Dwight. She simply could not.

Carolyn rested her head against the poplar's slender trunk and tried to force herself to breathe slowly. There had to be something she could do. But what? She had been so wrong and had made so many mistakes. When she had first arrived in Goudot, she had thought that coming to France had been a mistake. She wouldn't believe that. She had been meant to come here, and in a small way, she had helped the war effort. That wasn't a mistake. But so much else had been.

Carolyn stared into the distance, remembering the hospital in Goudot. She saw the patients laughing at her clothespin and Dwight's disapproval that somehow turned into a smile. There was Dwight in the operating theater, his eyes sparkling with pleasure when he and she saved a man's life. And Dwight on Christmas Day, dancing for the patients and laughing at the picture on a tin of toffees. Dwight. It all came back to Dwight.

Carolyn closed her eyes in pain, then forced them open again. She couldn't stop the memories on Christmas Day. She had to remember it all, and maybe then she would know what she had to do. Even though remembering meant facing her mistakes, she had to continue.

Carolyn watched raindrops slide down the tree trunk the way tears had slid down her cheeks when she had learned of Ed's death. She had made a major mistake that day, rejecting Helen's offer of help and hurting Dwight by rejecting his proposal. Theo was right. Ed wouldn't have wanted her to throw her life away. He had told her that he wanted her to be happy, but Carolyn hadn't listened. As a result she wasn't happy. Even worse, she was making everyone around her unhappy. What a fool she had been! Instead of seeking it, she had run from happiness.

Carolyn stared into the distance, trying to make sense of her jumbled thoughts. Admitting she had made a mistake was the first step, but it wasn't the last. She needed to undo her mistakes, or she would soon be left with nothing but regrets.

The question was, could she? Could she undo them?

Carolyn shuddered, thinking of the path ahead of her. Dwight had told her she was strong. He was wrong. She hadn't been strong, and that was one of her mistakes. She had let herself be buffeted by life's waves when she should have fought back. She should have swum against the tide if she had to, rather than let herself be pulled in the wrong direction, taking others with her.

Carolyn gripped the tree as she faced the biggest mistake she had made. Ed. Agreeing to marry him had not been a mistake. It had been the right thing to do at the time. The mistake was in not telling Ed how she felt about Dwight. Even when he had sensed it from her letters, Carolyn had denied her feelings. She had lied to Ed, and that had been wrong. She had thought she was protecting him. Instead, she had hurt Ed, and in the process, she had hurt herself and Dwight. That was the mistake.

Ed had been strong; he would have understood if Carolyn had told him that she *loved* him but was *in love* with Dwight. He would have released her from the engagement. Why hadn't she realized that? If she had been honest with Ed, she wouldn't feel so guilty. It was the lies she had told and the fact that she hadn't trusted Ed to understand that had filled her with remorse and made his death more painful.

Carolyn closed her eyes for a long moment, remembering the years she had known Ed. For the first time in weeks, his image was clear. She saw him laughing at the scrapes they'd gotten into. She heard him singing Christmas carols with her family. She felt his arms around her the day they had become engaged and remembered the sweet taste of his lips on hers.

Though the rain continued to pelt the ground, turning the earth to mud, Carolyn felt as if a cloud had lifted. Why had she been unable to see the truth that was now so clear? Ed was her friend; he was an important part of her past, but he was not part of her future. Denying her own chance at happiness would not bring Ed back. It was not what he would have wanted. It was, quite simply, wrong.

Carolyn took a deep breath and brushed the tears from her face. She could not undo the mistakes she had made with Ed or the hurt she had caused him. But maybe, just maybe, she could right one wrong. Maybe she could undo the mistakes she had made with Dwight.

Carolyn looked at her left hand, then slowly removed her glove. Even in the rain, the diamond sparkled, a reminder of the sparkle she had seen in Ed's eyes the day he had placed it on her finger. She would never forget that day, just as she would never forget Ed. But both were in the past. With hands that were surprisingly steady, Carolyn slid the ring from her finger and placed it in her pocket. Then she headed back to the hospital and her future.

Chapter Fourteen

Dwight awoke with a start, his heart pounding, his mouth dry with fear. He had been dreaming of her again. Reaching for the carafe that always sat on his nightstand, he poured himself a drink of water, then smiled ruefully as he realized that he was reacting like a physician, trying to reassure an anxious patient with a semblance of reality. He took a sip, then shook his head, not surprised when the fear that clutched his heart did not disappear.

It wasn't unusual to dream of Carolyn. He did that every night without fail. But this time had been different. The other dreams had been of her here in Goudot, dancing for the patients, shopping for Christmas gifts, joking with the men in the wards. They were always happy dreams that made him awaken wishing the dream would never end. But this was one Dwight hoped would never be repeated, for he had seen Carolyn in a strange place, sobbing as if her heart were breaking. Worst of all, he felt her despair and an almost overwhelming sense of loneliness because there was no one to share her sorrow, to help comfort her.

Dwight rose and began to pace the floor. Thank goodness the other doctors had not yet returned from their poker game. His roommates would surely have protested this noc-

188

turnal rambling. It wasn't difficult to understand why he had dreamed of Carolyn sobbing. The story of what had happened to Theo's company had reached Goudot yesterday. Being closer to the front, Carolyn would have heard it earlier. Of course she would be devastated.

Dwight clenched his fists, picturing Carolyn's face as someone—some well-meaning stranger—told her that her brother was dead. Had she begun crying immediately, or was the wound so deep that she had been in shock, unable to react until later when the pain broke through the barriers Nature had erected? Whenever reality had hit, it must have had the force of a speeding train. First her fiancé, now her brother. Poor Carolyn! How much could one woman, even one as strong as Carolyn, endure?

Dwight strode to the other side of the room, turned and marched back. Pacing was supposed to relieve tension. Hadn't he told patients that, urging them to repetitive motions? He had told women to knit, men to pace. It wasn't working. His thoughts were still as jumbled as when he'd wakened. He could still taste his fear. He could still picture Carolyn's grief.

Dwight executed another turn and strode back to the door. For a few minutes, he forced himself to think of nothing other than putting one foot in front of the other. This was what he had counseled patients. *Empty your mind. Concentrate on the mechanics of walking.* Had his patients found the advice as useless as he did?

Dwight wasn't sure how long he paced. All he knew was that one time when he approached the door, the image in his mind changed. Instead of Carolyn sobbing over Theo, Dwight pictured her face the last time he had seen her. There had been tears in her eyes then, and he had been the one who had caused them.

What a fool he had been! Dwight stopped in the middle of the floor, his shoulders sagging from the weight of his guilt. His problem wasn't Carolyn; it was himself and his pride. He had let his pride stand in the way of happiness. He had been hurt by her refusal to marry him. What man wouldn't be? But he had let his bruised pride overrule his common sense. He had lashed out, so hurt by what Carolyn wouldn't give him—marriage—that he had rejected what she could offer—friendship. Friendship wasn't everything Dwight wanted, but it was better than what he had now, which was nothing. Even his pride was gone, and in its wake was nothing but sorrow. Worse, his foolish pride had hurt the woman he loved more than anything on earth.

Dwight raised his head and straightened his shoulders. He knew what he had to do. She might reject him again, refusing even to be his friend. That was a distinct possibility and a painful one. But it was a chance he had to take. He had to try again, even though it meant risking his pride. He loved Carolyn; he needed her, and he believed she needed him.

Dwight thought quickly. Though his instincts told him to leave immediately, he knew that there would be a large number of wounded men arriving this morning. The hospital was already short-handed. If he left, his colleagues would be overworked and men might die. Dwight couldn't let that happen. But tonight after they had treated all the new patients, it would be different. Tonight he could go to Carolyn.

Carolyn hoped her smile didn't look as artificial as it felt. With each mile that passed, she felt her anxiety grow, and with each mile, it became more difficult to pretend that this was an ordinary journey.

She looked at the men who had been entrusted to her care and smiled again. If it hadn't been for them, she might have given in to her fears and turned around. Of course, Carolyn reflected with a wry smile, it was difficult to force a train to turn around.

When she had told the matron that she wanted to return

to her base hospital, the woman had merely nodded and said that she had expected the request and that she understood how painful it would be to be so close to the front under the circumstances. Since the matron had agreed that she could leave, Carolyn did not correct her assumption that the reason for the request was Theo's death.

The matron had pulled out a piece of paper and nodded again, telling Carolyn that a hospital train was heading from the front to Goudot that night. If Carolyn wished, she could travel on it. The staff on the train would be grateful for another nurse.

Carolyn was grateful for the opportunity. Treating the wounded men had helped her keep her fears at bay throughout the night. Though several of the doctors had raised eyebrows in what might have been either surprise or censure, Carolyn had joked with the patients. She hadn't planned to; the quips had simply slipped out along with some of her fictitious grandmother's sayings. It was, Carolyn told herself, a positive omen. This was the first time since she had left Goudot that she had been able to laugh, and oh, how healing that laughter had been. It had convinced her that she had made the right decision in planning to return to Goudot. Even more important, as they had laughed, the patients had started to relax. Nothing could change the fact that many of them were seriously wounded and that some would not make it home, but for a few minutes, their fear was lessened.

And so was hers. But now as they approached the station in Goudot, it returned, more powerful than ever. Carolyn could taste it, and she could feel the way her heart thudded, pumping dread through her body. What if he . . . ? No! She wouldn't think about that. She was doing what she had to do. Surely it would turn out all right.

"So what does your granny say about this hospital?" one of the men asked as the train began to slow for the station.

The train jerked, and Carolyn lost her balance. It was

only by grabbing a pole that she managed to keep from falling onto the floor. When she was once more upright, she grinned at the man who'd asked the question. "I reckon she'd tell me to count my blessings that the hospital is stationary."

The men laughed. One of them held up his hand and began to turn down each finger. "I'm counting my blessings," he told another.

Though she made no outward sign, Carolyn was counting her blessings, too. They had arrived. Dwight was here. And maybe . . .

"Nurse Clothespin!" The orderly who met the train couldn't hide his surprise. "I didn't know you were coming back."

Carolyn shrugged as she climbed down the iron stairs and helped a patient into one of the waiting wagons. It was only a short walk from the station to the hospital. If she started now, she could reach the hospital before the wagons were loaded with patients. She could see Dwight that much sooner. It was a tempting thought, but Carolyn would not desert the men she had cared for all night. "I just decided to come back yesterday," she told the orderly. "I need to get these men to the operating theater."

"Yes, ma'am."

The sky had lightened almost imperceptibly as the train had approached Goudot. Now, though the day remained cloudy, it was officially dawn. Carolyn closed her eyes for a moment, remembering how Ed and Theo had described the pleasure of climbing out of the trenches each morning at dawn. Neither of them would see another dawn.

Carolyn forced a smile onto her face. Though there would always be an empty place in her heart caused by the loss of Theo and Ed, crying now would do no good and would only upset the men she had tried to cheer.

Think of the future, Carolyn, she admonished herself. *Think of Dwight*, she repeated as she accompanied the men

to the operating theater. The man she thought about and
dreamed about was intent on suturing a wound when Carolyn entered the room where they had spent so many hours
together. She knew that look on his face. Until he had taken
the final stitch, nothing short of an earthquake would attract
his attention.

Holding a finger in front of her lips in the universal sig-
nal for silence, Carolyn tapped the assisting nurse on the
shoulder. "Let me," she mouthed. Though the woman's
eyes widened in surprise when she recognized Carolyn, she
nodded and flashed Carolyn a conspiratorial grin.

"Another suture." Dwight spoke without looking up, his
hands moving with the grace and assurance Carolyn had
always admired.

The operating room was filled with patients and staff.
The clank of instruments against metal, the sounds of soft
moans and firm commands, the smells of antiseptic and
infection told Carolyn this was an ordinary morning. And
yet it was not. For her, this was most definitely not an
ordinary morning.

Carolyn felt her pulse accelerate. It would be only seconds before Dwight saw her. What would he do? Would
he order her out of the operating room? It was possible
after the way she had hurt him that he would not want to
speak to her. Carolyn struggled to keep a smile on her face.
She couldn't give in to her fears. That would be another
mistake.

Wordlessly, she handed Dwight the suture he had requested. Perhaps he recognized her hands. Carolyn wasn't
sure. All she knew was that something caused him to look
up. She saw the recognition in his eyes and something else,
a fire that she couldn't identify. Was it anger? Or was it
something else? *Please*, she prayed silently, *let him not be
angry. Let him still care. Let him . . .* She took a deep
breath, then allowed herself to think the words that had

haunted her ever since she had told him good-bye the last time. *Let him still love me.*

When Dwight finished suturing the wound, Carolyn bandaged it as she had so many other wounds in the past. The lethargy that had plagued her at the field hospital was gone, replaced by an undeniable sense of excitement and accomplishment. Along with the pain of grief she carried everywhere, it also felt good to be back here, working with Dwight again.

As Carolyn prepped the next man for surgery, he gave her an imploring look. "Don't let him take my arm." The soldier gestured toward Dwight, who was studying his chart.

Carolyn managed a reassuring smile. "Doctor Hollins is the best. If anyone can save your arm, it's him." She kept her gaze on the patient's face, willing him to believe her. Confidence and a positive attitude were powerful weapons in the healers' arsenal. Perhaps if she could convince this man, she could also convince herself that today would have a happy ending.

"I bet you say that to everybody."

Carolyn heard the doubt and fear mingled in the patient's voice. "My granny taught me not to lie." The small sound that came from Dwight's direction might have been a snicker. Carolyn ignored it. What was important now was helping the man on the stretcher. "Granny said a liar was like a week-old fish." As she had hoped, the man's eyes, which had been clouded with apprehension, brightened at her analogy. "Everyone can smell it, and no one wants it around."

This time, there was no doubt that Dwight was laughing. So, too, was the patient. "You sure don't smell like no fish," he said. "You smell better than a bunch of flowers, so I reckon you're not lying."

Carolyn made a mocking curtsey. "Thank you for the compliment, kind sir. Now, you just relax." Although he did, she could not, for she knew what was ahead. While she wanted the shift to end so that she could talk to Dwight, at the same time Carolyn dreaded the prospect. What would she do if he refused her?

For the next few hours, she worked mechanically, handing Dwight the instruments he needed, joking with the patients when she could, trying desperately not to think of what she would say when the last of the men was treated. At times, she felt almost as if she had never left, but she had, and that made a difference. Though she and Dwight still worked well together, there was an undeniable distance between them that had not been there before.

Margaret was right. Carolyn had changed. They all had. Change didn't have to be bad. Carolyn knew that, and yet she could not dismiss the fear that Dwight had changed so much that he no longer loved her. She wouldn't think of that. Not now. What mattered now was helping Dwight save these men.

When the last patient was wheeled out of the operating theater, Carolyn turned to Dwight. "I need to talk to you." To her chagrin, the words came out almost like a croak. She hadn't realized how difficult it would be to pronounce such a simple sentence, but her throat had closed, refusing to let the sounds escape.

Though Dwight looked at her, she could read nothing in his expression. The hazel eyes that had haunted her dreams were hooded, and his lips were set in a straight line, neither frowning nor smiling. "Certainly," he said. "Shall we go to the lounge?" He might have been speaking to a post for all the emotion he displayed.

In the past, they would have spoken as they walked through the hallway. Today they were silent. Carolyn's heart was beating as fast as a hummingbird's wings, making her wonder whether she would be able to force a word through her lips. *Calm down*, she admonished herself as she tried to keep her breathing deep and regular. She couldn't give in to panic. Not now.

By some small miracle, the lounge was empty, and they moved instinctively, or so it seemed to Carolyn, to the chairs that they had occupied so many times in the past. When they were seated, Dwight leaned forward ever so slightly. His expression no longer inscrutable, she saw sympathy in his eyes. "I heard about your brother," Dwight said gently. "I wish there were something I could say to ease your pain."

Carolyn gripped the chair arms, trying to gather strength. Who would have thought this would be so difficult? She had never dreamed that baring her heart would tax her physically as well as emotionally. "Theo's not the reason I'm here." She took a deep breath, exhaled, then took another. She didn't expect Dwight to make this easy on her, not after the way she had rejected him, but Carolyn prayed that he would listen and understand. She met his gaze, hoping he could read the sincerity in her eyes. His own expression was once more unreadable. Though the grandfather clock chimed the hour, it was a measure of Carolyn's distress that she could not have said how many times it rang.

"I've done a lot of thinking since the last time we were together," she told Dwight. Somehow, the words came out clearly despite the turbulence of her thoughts. Dwight nodded, although Carolyn didn't know whether he was agreeing or simply encouraging her to continue. In either case, she had no choice. She had resolved that she would not stop until she had said everything that was in her heart. That was the only way she knew to try to correct her mistakes.

Carolyn tightened her grip on the chair as she continued to look at Dwight. "I know I hurt you, and that was wrong." Thank goodness, her voice no longer quavered. Though so much depended on Dwight's reaction, she would not let herself cry, for she wanted his love, not his pity. "Hurting you was one of the biggest mistakes I've ever made."

Dwight's eyes narrowed ever so slightly when he heard her admission. Though his lips remained in a straight line, he hadn't been able to hide the fact that her words had touched a cord inside him. Carolyn chose to regard that as a positive omen. At least he hadn't refused to listen to her. At least he seemed to care.

"I wish I could undo that day," Carolyn continued. "I know that's not possible, but . . ." She felt a moment of panic as her voice trailed off. Though Dwight was staring at her intently, she had no way of reading his thoughts. For a second, she was tempted to run away. She had known this moment would be difficult, but even her worst fears hadn't prepared her for the reality of facing Dwight, of opening her heart to him, of facing possible rejection. Was this how he had felt, each time he had asked her to marry him?

Carolyn swallowed deeply. She was not a coward, she told herself. She could do this. She had to do this. She swallowed again, then opened her mouth to ask the question whose answer would determine her future happiness. "Dwight, will you . . ."

Before she could complete the sentence, he interrupted. "Will I dance with you in the rain? Of course." A smile teased the corners of his mouth, and Carolyn took that as another good sign. If Dwight, the man whom the nurses had believed was born without the ability to smile, was now smiling, it had to be a positive omen.

"That was not what I was going to ask," she said. Her question was far more serious—and infinitely more important—than an invitation to dance in the rain.

As if he understood, Dwight nodded. Though the smile had disappeared, his eyes were no longer cool. Instead, they blazed with fire, a fire that began to warm Carolyn's heart.

"I hoped that wasn't your question," he said. He leaned

forward and took her hands in his. "Carolyn, I've made mistakes, too. I let my pride and anger take over. That was wrong."

His mistakes were nothing compared to hers. When Carolyn opened her mouth to tell him that, he shook his head slowly. "Let me," he said. For a moment Dwight was silent. He held her hands gently, and Carolyn knew that if she wanted to pull them away, he would not stop her. But she did not pull away. Instead, she tightened her fingers around his, trying to tell him without words that she never wanted to let him go. She would not reject his caress any more than she would reject him. That was one mistake she would not repeat.

Dwight looked down at their hands. When his eyes met hers again, Carolyn saw an emotion she recognized in them. Hope. Dwight hoped. So did she. Oh, how she hoped!

"I can't undo my mistakes any more than you," he said, "but perhaps we can put them behind us." Carolyn nodded, unable to speak. Was he going to say what she hoped he would? He had told her he would never say those words again, and yet there was no mistaking the emotion she saw blazing from his eyes.

Dwight smiled at her and said, "Carolyn, I love you."

They were the words she had wanted to hear. She had dreamed of this moment; the thought of it filled her waking hours; now, the warmth that flooded Carolyn's heart shocked her with its intensity. Three words, eight letters. Who would have dreamed that they held the power to heal so many wounds, to turn a day from gray to glorious, to make the future seem bright and shining?

"These last weeks have been horrible," Dwight said, his eyes closed with remembered pain. "I felt as if nothing had any meaning, because half of me was gone."

The look he gave her said he hoped she understood. Indeed she did. Carolyn swallowed, then found her voice. "I know. That's how I felt, too." The emptiness had been worse than anything she had felt before. When she had been alone in the past, she hadn't minded, but that had been before she knew how wonderful it was, being with Dwight. Dwight had made her complete; without him, she was only a shell.

He rose, tugging her to her feet, then looked down at her, his eyes once more serious. "I know I told you I wouldn't ask again, but I need to know. Do you love me, Carolyn?"

Surely he had never doubted that. But he had. His expression told her that he had not believed her when she had told him she loved him. All that he had heard was her rejection. Now was her chance to correct one of her mistakes.

Carolyn gripped Dwight's hands, willing him to believe what she was about to say. "Oh, Dwight, I love you. I love you more than I ever dreamed it was possible to love a person. I love you with all my heart." Carolyn looked into those hazel eyes that she loved so dearly, searching for a sign that he understood. Dwight's smile and the warmth that filled his eyes told her that this time he heard—and believed her.

"Then will you share all my tomorrows?" he asked. The note of uncertainty in his voice wrenched Carolyn's heart, for it was a measure of how deeply she had hurt him. Even now, when she had declared her love, he wasn't sure of her response.

She smiled and nodded, her heart so filled with emotion that she wasn't sure she could speak. But she had to. She had to ensure that Dwight knew she would never again reject him. "There's nothing I want more," she told him.

To Carolyn's surprise, he chuckled. "There's something I want more. I want to marry you." Dwight's face turned serious again. "Will you marry me, Carolyn?"

This time, there was no hesitation. "Yes, my darling! I want to marry you more than anything on earth."

As she moved into Dwight's arms and turned her face up for his kiss, the happiness that had been building inside Carolyn burst forth like water from a broken dam, flooding her with a joy deeper than anything she had ever experienced. No matter what the future brought, nothing could take away this moment, for in this moment, Carolyn had found her heart's desire: the man she would love for the rest of her life, the man who could turn sorrow to happiness, the man who would laugh with her as they danced in the rain.

Dear Reader,

I hope you enjoyed Carolyn and Dwight's story and that you're as anxious as I am to spend more time with the Wentworth family. *Dancing in the Rain* is the first of a trilogy, each featuring one of the Wentworth sisters.

Although both Carolyn and Martha believe that Theo has been killed along with the rest of his company, Emily refuses to accept that. Like many twins, she and Theo have always shared a special closeness. You can call it closeness, intuition or simply a bond between twins. Whatever it is, it's telling Emily that her brother is still alive. To prove that, she travels to France, where she meets Grant Randall, a newspaper correspondent who helps her conquer her fears by whistling in the dark. As they cross the war-torn countryside in search of Theo, Emily discovers that Grant has fears of his own, fears that threaten both of his happiness and hers.

I hope you'll join me for Emily and Grant's story, *Whistling in the Dark,* which should be available in early 2004.

Happy reading,
Amanda Harte